For Janet and Rich—
Here's to '67, the
production year!
Love,
Doug

# The King Diaries

# DOUGLAS MOON

*The King Diaries*

## McGRAW-HILL BOOK COMPANY

NEW YORK   TORONTO   LONDON   SYDNEY

for Martha

# The King Diaries

# Preface

As everyone who lived in San Francisco after World War I knows, the Lawrence Kings were an extremely prominent and well-to-do family, who, I am very proud to say, contributed most of the funds toward building the Church of the Respectable Light, over which I have happily presided for a number of years. There is no need to say that this was but one of their many, if not always wisely chosen, charities.

Equally well-known is the sad event which marked, how shall I say, the decline of this proud family: the lamentable, mysterious, and tragic disappearance of Lawrence King, head of the family, husband to the late Josephine and father to the late Edward King. I need not here go into great and, for me, painful detail regarding the behavior of the two Kings who survived Lawrence. It is common knowledge that his disappearance so affected them that they totally withdrew from the world into the confines of their own house, never to be seen again outside of it or by anyone inside of it, except myself.

If the reader is not familiar with these events, he will no doubt be astonished at such behavior, which, if I may

1

draw the parallel, is not unlike that of the early Christians, living in an Age of Darkness caused by the decay of Roman morals. One cannot imagine the surprise and horror of the Kings' many, many friends and associates—they had no living relatives—people who had had daily social and commercial intercourse with them, people who admired, respected, and, I dare say, loved them. All were simultaneously excluded save, as I have said, myself. To me only was their door opened and on me alone fell the thankful burden of taking care of their everyday needs, small as they became.

Of course, I did not and do not to this day condone unorthodox behavior; I believe that even so noble a feeling as grief can be carried to extremes, and that to do so is not in accordance with the Divine Will. That the Kings' behavior was extreme cannot be denied, and I can only lament that my continuous pleading with them to amend their way of life was without avail. Indeed, I was told by them at one point that, if I broached the subject again, I, too, should be forever excluded. I had no choice but compliance to this awful ultimatum, since I did not feel that, in turning their eyes from the world, they should also be allowed to turn them from God. Thus, I became their personal chaplain as well as their legal advisor and Man Friday, as it were.

The diaries themselves came into my hands in diverse ways. Edward King presented his to me on the afternoon before the tragic fire which destroyed the King house and the Kings in it. Mrs. King's diary was found, undamaged, in what had been the library safe. The portion of her diary printed here is a continuation of a longer diary which, I believe, she kept from the time of her husband's disappearance or, perhaps, before. The earlier volumes, and they must have been numerous, were apparently destroyed in the conflagration, for the safe contained nothing but the one volume, which begins midway through the entry which precedes that of March 28, 1960.

Edward's diary is printed in full. His first entry, April 1, 1960, antedates the fire by exactly one year, a strange coincidence.

## II.

Since I can make no claim that either diary has any enduring literary merit, the reader may well ask why I have spent the time and effort to have them published. My purpose is really quite simple. I hope that the diaries will somehow help to justify the ways of the Kings to those who once knew them. I feel this should be done, and I can think of no better way to do it than to follow John Milton's example in justifying the ways of God to Man and let the principals speak for themselves. To what better purpose could I put some of the money which their untimely deaths brought into my hands?

However, should this small tome fall into the hands of anyone who did not know the Kings, it will probably prove very dull reading. Indeed, some of the contents of both diaries is incomprehensible to me. This is attributable, I think, to the unfortunate turn of mind taken by Edward after the disappearance of his father and to the fact that only a fraction of Mrs. King's diary remains.

## III.

In all fairness to the reader, I must admit that many of my friends and colleagues have suggested that I abandon this endeavor altogether. Some of them object to the many eccentricities contained in both diaries, and all, with right on their side, object to the many, flagrant obscenities used by Edward. I would, indeed, be a poor and contemptible representative of my calling if I did not share these objections. And, to be sure, I do. However, I believe that the strength of these objections can be significantly lessened if steps are taken to eradicate, or at least disguise, the objectionable material so that only one already familiar with such things would be able to recognize it. This I have done through the use of asterisks.

I have not, however, transformed the objectionable words entirely into asterisks, since I saw no reason why "d*mn" should be mistaken for a more obscene word of four letters. (The average reader can, I am certain, think of several such which refer to sexual and excretory functions.)

One further word of warning before I close this already too lengthy and hurried Preface. Young people and those whose minds are not of the firmest should not, I think, be allowed to peruse this volume, for several reasons: Firstly, since young people cannot have known the Kings, many of Josephine King's allusions will be meaningless to them, and secondly, the strange and often unhappy thoughts of Edward King might tend to unsettle the minds of both the young and the infirm.

Finally, it is my expressed hope that in publishing these diaries—I shall offend no one, especially those guardians of the public morals who were so kind as to offer me their considered opinions.

ALFRED SYLVESTER PERKINS, D.D.
*San Francisco, California*
*August 16, 1965*

Where I have thought it advisable, I have annotated both diaries. Rather than place these notes at the end of each entry or all together at the conclusion of the book, I thought it would be more convenient for the reader if I incorporated them directly into the text. I have also had them printed in a type face slightly larger than that of the diaries so they will be easily distinguishable. It is my sincere hope that these notes, so printed, will not destroy the continuity of the text, where there is continuity, and that they will be as helpful to the reader as I intended they should be.

In one of these notes I explain my editorial relationship to the diaries. I should, perhaps, reiterate that policy briefly in this postscript. In short, I have made no grammatical, syntactic, or semantic changes in the text whatsoever. My emendations, such as they are, consist entirely of standardization in punctuation, capitalization, and, where I found it necessary, in orthography. I have already made note of the asterisk substitutions.

A. S. PERKINS, D.D.
*Biarritz, France*
*September 10, 1965*

UNDATED. [THE CONTINUATION OF AN EARLIER VOLUME. *Mrs. King.*]

. . . trials and tribulations of an aging woman who hopes she is dear to her son,

[Mrs. King's style is peculiar to herself. She writes in the third person singular, as did Caesar, combined with the first person plural of newspaper editors and royal personages. That the first person singular pronoun "I" never appears in her narrative is a lasting tribute to her modesty, although her unprecedented mixture of the two other persons may temporarily confuse the reader.]

God's only recompense to her for continuing years of unmitigated suffering. Therefore, have we decided that she is to rest in the afternoons, an event never heard of before in her career, an event which will deprive her of several hours of the blissful comforts of her soul's shepherd,

[A very kind reference to me.]

but which will, we hope, assist her in successfully maintaining the burden of enlivening the existence of those few left who are still dear to her, namely that same shepherd and her only begotten son, Edward, dearest of the dear.

We are reminded of several heroines of radio fame

[Mrs. King had always been a great admirer of the radio. However, by the time this entry was made, there was no functioning set in the house. The console had ceased to work some five years before. Mrs. King would not allow me to have it repaired, nor would she hear of having a new one brought into the house. She was thus deprived of one of her few pleasures in life.]

who suffered in similar proportions; and we hope that she can and will benefit from their similar experiences. Raising a son, orphaned by fate, is no easy burden to place on the shoulders of a frail woman,

[Mrs. King perhaps exaggerates her condition. To the best of my knowledge, she entertained perfect health throughout the course of her life, which was all to the good, since I do not believe she would have seen a medical doctor, even in the direst necessity.]

a woman frail in stature, in health, and made more frail by being pampered, yet not spoiled, in her youth. Can she succeed, will she, ought she? Will fate deprive her of her son or her son of her? These questions have long bothered her; a graying head should not be so molested, but so molested should not succumb either to apathy or despair. On this tragic note, we must close our brief vignette, remembering always to hope for and expect improvements where none appears forthcoming.

MARCH 28, 1960. [*Mrs. King*].


We cannot but wonder how her son will accept the news.

["News" refers to Mrs. King's intention of informing Edward that she, with my help, had decided to take a nap in the afternoon. This rest was thought advisable because she frequently had trouble sleeping at night. It would certainly be a thoughtless son who could deny his mother so simple and salubrious a request.]

Surely he will understand that a woman in her years of decline, yea, fall, has needs foreign to the young and lively. Can he begrudge her a few hours repose, repose which she hopes will make her a more fitting companion for one but half her age? Can her action be construed as selfishness when viewed in this light?

These questions haunt us like the ghosts of murdered martyrs. But what other course? Whither? We hope that he may learn to employ to good purpose these extra hours left him by her absence. Thus, have we suggested that he, following her maternal example, will learn to record his thoughts on paper, not so much that they may be read by posterity, but that they will occupy him in time of leisure, for idle hands are an invitation to the devil.

[Although an eccentric woman, I do not believe that Mrs. King ever wavered in her faith. Her piety, although she regrettably did not attend church, remained one of her foremost virtues.]

The good Reverend, heaven be praised, agrees with her plan and says she must mention it to her son as soon as is humanly possible. Perhaps tomorrow or the day after, when we have gathered our strength and developed a persuasive, yet gentle, framing for the proposal.

[Her tender regard for her son also was one of her foremost virtues.]

The heroines of radio fame were confronted with greater obstacles, more serious dilemmas, and more imposing tasks. Oh, may he not employ these hours in the wine cellar,

[This fear seems somewhat misplaced, since Edward never exhibited any tendency toward this dread affliction. He was, I am almost certain, a total abstainer.]

hitherto sealed for the past ten years.
God grant her a *modus operandi!*

[Latin, literally, "method of operation" or, more correctly, "of operating." It refers here to the manner in which Mrs. King planned to inform her son that she wished to take a nap in the afternoon.]

Alas, my a*s, the beloved one is asleep upstairs, Her first nap, saith she, since the days of childhood and Robinhood. And SHE IS A LIAR for she has only exchanged her chair, the dozing rose of yesteryear, for a bed.

> [Mrs. King, as I have mentioned, informed me about this time that she felt the need for an afternoon nap. I, of course, recommended that she see a doctor. My visits hereafter ended at three in the afternoon, rather than at four.]

Old age, saith she, makes her sleepy and she needs her nap. So I am left to myself and my own devices. Flatulent F*rt

> [I assume this jocular reference is to me, since no one else visited them, as I mentioned in the Preface. To be sure, Edward never so addressed me to my face. He usually called me "the Reverend Doctor Perkins," although at this time I had not yet received my Doctorate in Divinity.]

does not come today. Thank G*d and G*d and G*d, thus working in the trinity. Ah, peace! And so I shall follow the proffered example—not as I do, but as I say—of the beloved and write little letters to myself, letters not to be read by readers—as hers are intended to be, for she is a dear heart and a simple—but, alas, my a*s, to be written and not even reread, to write away the hours till Beauty is kissed by the Handsome

One and again returns to life. May Friendly F\*rt keep his distance until Thursday when we shall all have our Merry Tea in the Drawling Room. God must not be meeting the standards of inflation. Sunday came he—our angel of mercy—to say that we should sell something or other preferred,

> [It was my custom to transact all the family business. Mrs. King had given me power of attorney nine years earlier. Edward was usually impatient and sometimes scornful about such matters. His attitude did not make my job any easier.]

be it T\*rd Preferred, and buy something common, Common Wh\*re. Or else our little nest egg might not hatch. Many are the ways of the Lord and more are the ways of his servants. Amen. Old Fairly Ferocious F\*rt almost looked as if he were going to open the Topic Forbidden. Oh, let him try it. How much pain it will cause him to be told that he is no longer needed—

> [I cannot believe that Edward ever seriously considered suspending my services, nor was it in his power to do so.]

how much pleasure to tell him. Would she would consent, Conservative Stick. But she must have her thrice weekly teas. A remanent of a world beyond the walls—ten years, ten thousand miles beyond. Ten F days

> [This reference is lost on me. It may have something to do with the disappearance of Lawrence King, which preceded this entry by nearly ten years. Mr. King was never mentioned by his son, and Mrs. King never discussed him after giving me power of attorney.]

beyond, and coming again in June, the month of many brides and fewer maidenheads. An hour to go and then upstairs to *maman*, her human alarm clock—Prince Charming, Bed Warming. No T*rd Preferred till Thursday. Yesterday she says to me, "Edward, you should keep a diary." "Madame," say I, "Cows would muss the carpet." "Silly boy," says she, "one only makes that mistake in writing. It will do you good. Clear the cobwebs out of your fine brain and give us something else in common. Tee Hee." "But, madame," say I, "what is writing?" "Writing," says she, "is writing." "No, I beg to differ," say I "writing is righting!" And so she won again, G*d d*mn it, but never shall she know. I will say I spend the time reading those horrible magazines which Fructuous F*rt brings to draw us out of ourselves—

[Unfortunately, this little ruse failed.]

the back issues in the cellar. Thousands of them. Three feet deep—but not the special stacks and I will tell her this today. Two hours already—and a slow process this and dull. Into the Spode with you, you slave-driver.

[This apparently refers to a soup tureen which sat on a buffet in the unused dining room. On that fateful day mentioned in the Preface, Edward King asked me into that room and, fetching the diary out of the tureen, gave it to me for safe-keeping.]

APRIL 5, 1960. [*Mrs. King*].


Her darling boy has kept her so occupied every waking hour that she has not had time to make her daily entries.

[This I take to exhibit Edward's fundamental thoughtfulness in regard to his mother. It is certainly a quality to recommend him.]

We wonder if this will continue.

[It apparently did to some degree, since it seems that prior to April she was not in the habit of letting three days pass together without an entry. Indeed, I have reason to believe that her entries had been made on a regular daily basis prior to March 28th. The lapse between March 28th and April 5th must be at least partially attributable to the confusion caused by so major a change in such an established routine.]

The attentions of the young are flattering, but she has a duty to herself and perhaps even to posterity, should any well-intentioned, humane person

[It, of course, gives me great pleasure that I was elected by Providence to this office. One wishes that Mrs. King's reflections had the desirable continuity of a work complete.]

ever see fit to publish these, the memoirs of an aging woman

14

who has tried to record her simple thoughts for the perusal and instruction of the young. Perhaps one day he will ask to read these little volumes himself. Perhaps he will ask her to read his if, indeed, he is keeping any, or rather, one. How thrilling to think on't, as Edward says the Shakespearians say. We have no idea: Where does he keep it if he is keeping one? How these trifles molest her brain, but has she not been through the house, every nook and cranny, as a dutiful mother should? How many minor pleasures and intrigues a small household can yield!

The good Reverend brought the case of rubbing alcohol

[To be sure, it always gave me a great deal of pleasure to do these little things for Mrs. King. For the record, as it were, it should be noted that this particular compound was not the normal iso-propyl or denatured ethyl alcohol normally used for medicinal purposes. It was Mrs. King's considered opinion that juniper had a salubrious effect on her sinuses and was thus in the habit of applying this compound, rather than the ordinary rubbing compound, to her back and shoulders. I admit that this always struck me as somewhat strange, but I was pleased to think that those bottles which I brought her would not find their way into hands which might put them to far worse use.]

for her complaint.

[What her exact complaint was I cannot say, since she was not in the habit of discussing her physical ailments with me. I suspect, however, that it might have been something in the line of a mild arthritis or rheumatism, since she once mentioned an application to back and shoulders. She was blessed in that no outward symptoms of either disease manifested themselves on her person.]

Never thinking but thinking of others, is the good Reverend. But he must not trouble himself so. What business could she and her son have with a new apartment? So long have they been established in a homestead, like pioneers. We cannot so easily desert tradition, and we hope the good Reverend Mr. Perkins does not mention the subject again. It so troubles her and her son. Surely, the good man exaggerates when he says the neighborhood is declining.

[The neighborhood was and still is in a state of decline, although Mrs. King, recluse that she was, could not be expected to observe it. What once had been fine old family homes are now mainly multi-dwelling units occupied by certain unfortunate minority group members in the lower income range. People who live on property which they do not own cannot be expected to care for it in the same way as people who do.]

Although she does not leave the house, she could certainly see traces of this decline, if it is so apparent as the good Reverend says. Perhaps he thinks the house too large for two and perhaps too dusty. And her neighbors, even though communication has ceased, would not Mr. Silas Croft

[Of Mr. Croft I know very little, since he belonged to a denomination other than my own: Unitarian, I believe. It is somewhat strange that Mrs. King should have exhibited such concern for him, since I believe that before the disappearance of Mr. King, they were not, how shall I say, on social terms. I have heard it said that Mr. Croft's real name was Kraft and that he

16

made his money (a fortune of nearly two millions) in Frankfurt, Germany before coming to the United States of America. How true this is I cannot say.]

dislike having new people next door? Has he not lived there even longer than she has lived here? How these problems plague her, and where are we to turn? She is too upset to continue.

APRIL 6, 1960. [*Edward King*].

This diary business is a pain in the a*s. So I told Her I was reading magazines in the cellar and so I have been for the past five days, every day from three to five. *Post* magazines with paintings of everyone's happy family doing funny things. So I have been drawing teats on all the red-haired, fuckle-faced

[So reads the text, but I dare say Edward meant "freckle" or, more properly, "freckled."]

boys and erasing the blue eyes of all the little blond girls and drawing hardons on the little black and white spaniels. O Vulgar Occupation! And an idle one if I weren't planning to return them all to Saint Alfreda Perkinensis, Jove's cupbearer. The only pleasure I get out of this b*stard diary is following my besainted and bedeafening mother

[If Mrs. King were actually growing deaf at this time, she certainly showed no signs of it in her conversations with me. Perhaps Edward really means "deafening," indicating that his mother was not as circumspect as she might have been in her playful search for his diary.]

around in the morning while she hunts for it, a nobler and less idle occupation than improving the pious art of Norman Crockwell.

[This is probably not a misspelling, but an attempt at humor. I am certain that Edward was referring to

18

Norman Rockwell, an American artist who needs no explanation. A colleague of mine, who does not wish to be identified, suggested Norman Vincent Peale and Lincoln Rockwell. Norman Mailer was proposed and rejected when it was learned he is not a painter.]

Ganymede Perkins came yesterday with his monthly present of rubbing alcohol and we (*maman et moi*)

[What follows is nothing more than the fantasies of an idle and perhaps demented mind. I have not omitted it, or any like it, in the interest of completeness, but I strongly recommend that the delicate reader continue immediately to the next entry. Regrettably, this is not the last entry of this kind nor, I believe, the worst. If there is any justification for not omitting this passage other than the aforesaid completeness, it is to show that an idle mind may become as corrupted as idle hands. The only pleasure I can derive from such writing is the assurance that Mrs. King did not find her son's diary.]

got massaged last night and played Helen Trent. I made a magnificent Gil Stratton as usual. There I sat in my rose garden in the South (Mother insisting it's Southern California, the Shallow as opposed to the Deep South), mint julep in hand. I record here snatches of our dialogue for the edification of my following, my following of one, me. Ah yes, I will construct a little playlet, a toy all of my own making, a little toy, a toilet.

[Edward originally wrote "toylet." My dictionary has no such entry, so I have taken the liberty, no great one, surely, of changing the spelling to one which we all know, to a word the meaning of which has greatly deteriorated over the last century, or so says my dictionary. Let this serve as a warning to all who are not as careful with language as they might be.]

I will give my toilet a title, too: Some Snatches of Dialogue. I had considered "Dialogue of Some Snatches," but I rejected it for casting reasons. Any fool can see why.

[This may be true, but I fail to find any sense in the second title Edward mentions. This is probably why he rejected it. But what, we may wonder, does this have to do with casting?]

We find Gil, played by Edward King, sinking into a dusty, overstuffed lawn chair in his Attic rose garden.
GIL: Ah, G*d, Ah am exhausted. Ah just finished beatin' all mah male Negra he'p and rapin' all mah female Negra he'p. And here Ah find mahself awaitin' fur Helen Honey Mother to drive her li'l ol' *ss down here from the Big City. She-it.

[Two pronouns. What they are supposed to mean, hyphenated in this manner, is anyone's guess.]

(Helen-Mother pulls up the gravel-paved, rose-studded drive on her tricycle, the only mode of transportation available in the attic, excellent exercise, though.) T*rds and orange blossoms, Gil honey, I'm here. I see you're all crippled up as usual with arthritis, rheumatism, bursitis, poliomyelitis and what not. You look just like a pile of trash somebody dynamited, honey.
GIL: (He ignores her comment, recognizing it for what it really is, a pleasantry.) Hi thare, Helen honey, howdy, howdy. Y'all got a new car?
HELEN-MOTHER: Why, yes. I'm right glad you noticed. Right proud, as one of your Neegrows might say. I sold my '39 La-Salle Roadmaster Super de Luxe Coupe de Grass for a song.
GIL: Can y'all sing it for me, sweetie?

HELEN-MOTHER: G*d d*mn it, that's just an expression.

GIL: What is?

HELEN-MOTHER: "For a song," d*mn it! I didn't sell my car for a song. Good G*d, man, what kind of a nut do you think I am, working and slaving my fingers off to the bone in the Big City, and you, you d*mn fool, think I'll turn around and sell my car —my practically new car—for a G*d d*mned song. Jee-s*s Keyrist, h*ll, sh*t, and high water, Gil, honey. It's an expression.

[Mrs. King never spoke in this manner, ever.]

GIL: Oh, is that right? Well, what did y'all sell it fur, then?

HELEN-MOTHER: Fur because I wanted a new one, you dumb *ss. One of these three-wheeled jobs. (She revs up her motor and falls over into a pile of old curtains. There is a silent explosion of dust.) Where'd they go?

GIL: Who?

HELEN-MOTHER: The sheriff and his posse.

GIL: They don't come on till later.

HELEN-MOTHER: Oh.

GIL: So y'all ain't gonna sing to me after all?

HELEN-MOTHER: Well, I could. What would you like to hear, "Night and Day?"

GIL: How 'bout some li'l ol' thing y'all writ yourself up thare in Hollywood?

HELEN-MOTHER: All right. (She sings. The tune is irrelevant, unrecognizable, unmusical. Imagine the spontaneous reaction of a hyena and a crow who have unexpectedly been shat upon by a very sick bull elephant.)

> "Life beginneth at thirty-five,
> A pee-pee, pooh-pooh, piddle-O!
> It endeth not at thirty-four,
> A pee-pee, pooh-pooh, piddle-O!

It doesn't matter, you will thrive
If, like me, you're thirty-five,
Always, ever, thirty-five!"

GIL: Beautiful. Bee-YOU-tee-full. The refrain is particularly moving, purgative almost.
HELEN-MOTHER: (Sullenly.) I wasn't done. I had a whole nother stanza.
GIL: Well, sing it, honey.
HELEN-MOTHER: I need a little something to tide me over from my long journey down from the Big City first. (Gil hands her a mint julep: ⅘ quart Old Massage. Helen-Mother swallows ⅕ quart Old Massage, bats not an eye and belches.) Brapp. Thanks, honey. I ready. (She means "I'm ready." "I ready" is only meant to add a kind of baby talk, Betty Boop atmosphere.)

"I'm headed for the menopause
'Cause I'm as old as Santa Claus,
But I don't care a f*rt for that!
Come kiss my teeny, aging pratt.
A pee-pee, pooh-pooh, piddle-O!"

GIL: (Misty-eyed, moved.) Lovely, jus' lovely. More beautiful than "Ah! Sweet Mystery of Life."

[Only someone as callous and crude as Edward could even mention these two "songs" in the same breath. Personally, I could not count the number of peaceful hours that Victor Herbert's melody has given me. How many could?]

HELEN-MOTHER: "Yes, come kiss my teeny, aging pratt, Because . . ."
GIL: Honey, y'all gonna wear out that lovely li'l singin' voice of urine.

22

HELEN-MOTHER: (Undaunted.) "Because it's so . . ."

GIL: Mother!

HELEN-MOTHER: "Because it's so old and cute."

GIL: "A pee-pee, pooh-pooh, piddle-O!"

HELEN-MOTHER: Amen!

GIL: Honey?

HELEN-MOTHER: Yes?

GIL: 'Fore y'all got here, ah was asittin' here and awonderin', here in mah rose garden, if y'all, bein' as how y'er thirty-five and all, shouldn't retire down here with me on the floor and in mah rose garden. Yeah, how about that? Maybe trade in your tricycle, sorta get the lay of the land, heh, heh, and maybe buy a three speed wheel chair or somethin'. How 'bout that, sweetleums, pooh-baby lover?

(Modesty, yea, shame, forbids me to repeat Mother-Helen's comment on this simple request of Gil's. Let it suffice to say that poor Gil was told that rose-gardening suggested a deviant sexual orientation, that his physical condition suggested impotence, and that it would be easier for him to run a flag up a wet noodle than to do something else. Had he not but recently completed the rounds of the plantation help, he would certainly have cast aside his julep and proved the lady wrong on all three counts. Mother-Helen appreciated the sentiment, said some nice things about my Fine Southern Manhood, hoped that I could keep it alive, and fell headlong into the curtains and a long series of juleps, much deserved. But alas, she ended in tears, weeping for the good old days before the radio expired, passed away into the Great Silence in the Sky.

[Of course, I pleaded with Mrs. King on many occasions to allow me to have the radio repaired. She always objected but would not state her reasons. Edward once confided to me that it was because she was sentimental about the old tubes. I am afraid this is but some more of his wayward humor.]

23

'Twas a sight to rend even the most callous of hearts, had not the tenderest of hearts become immune. The Dearly Beloved One was forced to fall asleep in her tears amid the curtains because she could not walk to bed, and I was in no condition to carry her.

Tomorrow and tomorrow and tomorrow creeps in this petty

[This is a paraphrase from a play by William Shakespeare, the British dramatist.]

Perkins from day to day, so I think that I shall light my own way to the cellar and continue my art work. I cannot bear to hear how the neighborhood is declining from the flatulent lips of Tremulous Time, Man Girl-Scout.

APRIL 7, 1960. [*Mrs. King*].


[In this passage, as well as elsewhere, Mrs. King's
generally lucid style becomes somewhat obscure, this
being attributable, no doubt, to her frequent, if ex-
cusable, failure to edit. A learned colleague of mine
suggested that I undertake the editing myself, and I
must admit that I gave her suggestion due consideration, going so far as to reconstruct this particular passage. However, the results of my little endeavor bore
so little resemblance to the original that I immediately gave over, deciding rather to place my confidence in the interest and abilities of the reader. I
hope that I have not erred in this. To the doubting, I
can only say, as others have said before me, that the
style is often equated with the man.]


Dear Readers (if we are ever to be so fortunate as to have
any; but this, alas, is in the hands of Providence, for she will
not, but not out of modesty, attempt to make her little moral
vignettes public herself), you will be pleased to note that we
have only missed one day in sitting down to our little thoughts.
Such are the rewards of application. May they continue.

She has been doing a good deal of thinking the past day or
so about beginning life anew. Although she is long past the
"starting-over" age,


[I had no idea at this time that Mrs. King was so
taken by my suggestion. Had I known, I would, of

course, have pressed the matter much more strongly than I did.]

she has remembered the unparalleled example of a radio heroine, who shall here be anonymous, who felt or seemed to feel, as it were, that life could really begin at a more advanced age than it is generally conceded to begin at. This woman with a career (although we do not have a career, *per se,* we have raised an orphaned, either by fate or death, son which is a career in itself, being both father and mother and even, if you like, brother and sister) and a gentleman friend from the South, we do not know the exact state, who wanted very much to marry her but was himself incapacitated, the cause not being mentioned, decided that she could begin life, perhaps, by marrying again, which, of course, we could not do out of respect to her late husband, nor expect a stranger to accept the burden of a stepson.

[I have no objections, either personal or professional, to the remarriage of a legal widow, which Mrs. King was. Had she decided to remarry, Edward, who obtained his majority shortly before the disappearance of his father, would have presented little or no problem to his mother or his stepfather.]

If only the good Reverend were here to guide her. The excitement of possible change at an advanced age overcomes her.

Two hours later, dear friends.

[At least part of this two hour lapse seems to have been occupied in conversation with Edward. I have little doubt that he was instrumental in discouraging

26

the aforementioned plan. Certainly, if the charge of selfishness can be brought to bear on anyone, it is not Mrs. King.]

Careful thought and speculation have led her to reconsider such a momentous move, even with the most unparalleled example. There are in her case extenuating circumstances in the form of others

["Others" should probably be read "other," otherwise, it must be understood that I am included categorically as one who would have discouraged her. Such was not the case.]

besides herself to be considered. Let the kind reader be advised that one must always carefully examine their own motives, howsoever unselfish they may appear from outward appearances, to ascertain that there is no selfishness appearing from within. How could she expect her son, now grown, either because of fate or death, a veritable hermit, to go hence into a world unknown and unknowing, to begin a new life. Perhaps she will be accused of overprotection, for so sheltering him. However, must we not ask ourselves if the blow to a young mind occasioned by the death or disappearance of a father is not one blow too many? Could any mother, albeit even a callous one, expose a tender mind, made even more tender by one blow, to the possibilities of another one? Even if she herself is strong enough to go forward again herself, are there not others who would not follow?

[If the reader will forgive another intrusion, I would like to point out Mrs. King's almost saintly unselfishness. Could anyone hold up eccentricity as a vice against such a consummate virtue?]

27

These questions are not put well and they are not unanswerable as some which we have raised elsewhere.

These questions have shown her the answer, have pinpointed and illuminated a well of selfishness, and have forced her to come forth with a resounding negative to all questions hitherto asked. And is this not a painful experience? Here we must answer affirmatively with a fervent and profound hope that any reader, if there be any such, takes heed of her profitable experience and profits by it as well.

Nor does she place any blame whatever on any other person

[This I take to be an allusion to Edward, for it could be to no other person.]

who might have put any such ideas into her mind, for her mind is its own receptor and rejector and a sacred temple. It would be well if any reader would caution his own to be such as well. She is afraid that brevity will not draw the point so well as a longer and more reasoned discourse, but excitement and a hurried pen have exhausted her frail and aging body, and we can only hope that anyone wishing to miss the point, ill-made as it may be, will subject this passage to reperusal.

APRIL 8, 1960. [*Edward King*].


[It is quite possible that the following scene, which Edward presents in semi-dramatic form, may actually have taken place. Those parts of it which strike the reader as fantastic, or are repugnant, are the product, not of reality, but of Edward's active, if unhappy, imagination.]

"The Poor Dear One." Scene: the library. Enter Mother with pen and journal, Son with pack of cards. Mother seats herself at a table by the window and begins to write furiously in her diary. Son seats himself across the table from her and begins to play solitaire. Scene continues much the same for fifteen to twenty minutes. Mother bites end off pen, stands abruptly, flies out of the room, and is heard ascending several flights of stairs. Son watches her depart and continues to play at cards for two hours. Mother re-enters the room slowly, wearing toothy grin and wedding dress, vintage War of 1812. Son starts back and exclaims: Merrill Lynch, Pierce, Fenner and Chr*st, Mother!
MOTHER: Nay, Edward my son, do not be shocked. The good Reverend has convinced me that we must once again go forth into the world. (Son, convulsed with laughter, rolls around on the floor. Mother stands by undaunted and continues.) This is not a time for foolery. Many years ago when I was young, very young, and had no experience of the world, your father paid a visit to my father to arrange our marriage. I had never seen him before . . .
SON: Who, your father?

29

MOTHER: No, my husband.

SON: But I didn't think you were married yet.

MOTHER: I wasn't. You're not listening to me.

SON: Yes, I am. You had never seen him before.

MOTHER: Yes, I had never seen him before, but I put on this dress, and we were married and went out into the world together.

SON: You were both wearing this dress? (He fingers it.)

MOTHER: NOOO! The good Reverend . . .

SON: (Incredulous.) The three of you were wearing this dress?

MOTHER: (Pretending not to hear.) The good Reverend . . .

SON: The good Reverend Smell O'F*rt ought to have his little pink a*s kicked out to sea. I'm beginning to get the picture, the *wedding* picture.

MOTHER: This is no time for humor. Mr. Perkins has only the very best intentions. (Admires the dress.) I was a virgin when I first put on this dress, and I am not one now. To be sure, it was not Reverend Perkins who married us, he was only a small boy then, good man.

SON: So take off your dress, sexpot, I'm hungry for you.

MOTHER: No, Edward, this is a time to be serious.

SON: I *am* serious!

MOTHER: (Disapprovingly.) Edward!

SON: (Approvingly.) Mother!

MOTHER: (Giggling girlishly.) Edward! Be serious about our leaving this house and going to an apartment with a view, and getting jobs or something of that kind.

SON: Where would we go?

MOTHER: I don't know. The Reverend will find us a place.

SON: Perhaps we could live with him and polish pews. (He sings a few lyrics from "My Blue Heaven.")

MOTHER: No, I understand he has only a small cottage with one bedroom.

SON: We could all sleep together. Dibs on middles.

MOTHER: O, Edward, Edward. Shame, shame.

SON: (Singing.) Dame Shame and Friar Liar were Wheat Hearts eating sweethearts all in the merry, merry month of May.

MOTHER: April, not May.

SON: Point and counter point. *Touché*. April is the cruelest month breeding plans and parsons. Are we running out of money or something?

MOTHER: No, Mr. Perkins says we have too much.

[I am sure I did not word it in this way. I remember telling Mrs. King, when questioned by her, that she had more than she needed or would ever need.]

SON: Then why leave?

MOTHER: I don't know. It seemed like such a good idea. *Helen Trent* . . .

SON: Helen D*amnation! Wasn't Gil impotent? Did *he* leave *his* plantation? Did she drag him off to Hollywood to become a movie star? No, no, and again, No! I beseech you, Mother, and I have no other, let us be reasonable. Acquiesce!

MOTHER: I fear you may be right. It is no one's business but ours. Let us stay and be as we have been. (Son cheers, rushes up to Mother, tears off the dress and throws it into the fireplace. He lights it. It burns. Mother sobs once. Then laughs. She returns to her journal, he to his cards. She writes for fifteen minutes and closes the journal. They play honeymoon bridge for half an hour. A clock strikes twelve. An ambulance pulls up in front of the house. Mother stands up, obviously frightened. The ambulance moves slowly away and stops in front of Mr. Croft's house. Mother sits down, obviously relieved. Two laughing men in white suits step out of the ambulance and fetch a stretcher from the rear door. The three of them disappear into Casa

[Spanish for "house."]

31

Croft. Mother and Son watch anxiously for twenty to twenty-one minutes. The attendants and stretcher reappear. The former are bearing the latter, and the latter is bearing Mr. Croft or a reasonable facsimile thereof.)

EDWARD: Mr. Croft is going out into the world.

MOTHER: My G*d, I believe he's dead!

SON: Let's not jump to conclusions.

MOTHER: But what if he *is* dead?

SON: Then his soul is in the hands of the Angels.

MOTHER: We can't be sure. Mr. Perkins thinks he's . . . not a Christian.

SON: Mr. Perkins thinks too much.

MOTHER: He has to, Edward, he has a responsible position.

SON: Perhaps Mr. Croft did too.

MOTHER: Perhaps. I wonder if the house will be sold.

SON: He has no family.

MOTHER: Oh, Edward, we really should have been better neighbors.

SON: We can't be neighbors. We live in the same house, together, the two of us, just you and me.

MOTHER: No, I mean Mr. Croft.

SON: But he doesn't live here.

MOTHER: I know. He's dead.

SON: Yes.

MOTHER: I could have taken him some soup.

SON: But you don't go out of the house, Mother.

MOTHER: Mr. Perkins could have taken it then.

SON: Perky would have poisoned it.

MOTHER: Surely not.

SON: Maybe he took Mr. Croft some soup on his own.

MOTHER: No, Mr. Croft did not belong to Mr. Perkins.

SON: Out of Christian charity.

MOTHER: But Mr. Perkins doesn't think that Mr. Croft *is* a Christian. (The ambulance pulls away. Mother waves from behind the curtain.) Goodbye, Mr. Croft. We should have

32

been better neighbors. (Turns to Son.) I'm sure he's not really dead, Edward. It may just have been an attack of indigestion.

SON: From Perkins' poisoned potage?

MOTHER: No, Edward, from whatever it is that Mr. Croft eats.

SON: Maybe he starved to death.

MOTHER: (Returning to the cards.) Your deal, Lucille. (She giggles at her own marvelous rhyming joke.) We'll have to start over. I don't remember where we were.

SON: I said, maybe he starved to death.

MOTHER: (Somewhat uncomfortable.) I know. You sound like Reverend Perkins. No one has ever starved to death in this neighborhood. We should have heard about it. Now, deal.

SON: Yes, Mother.

(The Curtain Falls Because It
Is Thirty-Five Years Old And
The Two Are Left Exposed
To The Street.)

APRIL 10, 1960. [*Mrs. King*].


She has suggested to the good Reverend that he compose a sermon on the text, "Thou shalt love thy neighbor as thyself." The good Reverend said that he had taken this passage as a text many times and would be only too pleased to give her a manuscript copy of two of these and a printed copy of another, if she cared to peruse any of them.

> [This particular sermon, entitled, "Adultery: an Inquiry into the Metaphysics of Sin," is available in the *Quarterly Word*, Vol. LXI, iii. Two others on the same subject will soon appear in a collection entitled Alfred Sylvester Perkins, D.D., *An American Views the Ten Commandments* (All Hallows Press, Garth, Mississippi). For anyone interested in pursuing the subject further, I strongly recommend General Beaumont Bonaparte Buck's "Christ on Castro and the Cuban Crisis: A New Definition of Neighbor," *The Church Militant*, XXX, i, pp. 406–98. See also Wilhelm and Greta Goethe, "Defecting Gentiles and the Resurgence of Communism in America," *Freiheits Verlag*, I, i.]

Of course, the good man was puzzled as to the occasion of such a request, and she could not help but mention that the recent and lamented demise of a neighbor,

> [This neighbor, whom for some reason Mrs. King chose to leave anonymous, is Mr. Kraft, of course.]

who shall here be anonymous, albeit that he had no living relations or kin, has caused her to think that she, perhaps, had neglected him, he being a neighbor for nearly half a century or fifty years.

The good Reverend Mr. Perkins, for we think it only fitting here to name him, of course guessed whom we had in mind, and, thoughtful man, suggested that a new, short and personal sermon

[The sermon is quoted in full in the next entry.]

well might be more appropriate, considering that one is not sure exactly what the denomination of the good neighbor might have been or was. Tomorrow, if the good Reverend keep his word, she shall be able to transcribe the same into her little "Dictionary of Moral Vignettes," as she likes to think of it, for her further improvement and the improvement of anyone who might happen to stumble onto these little vignettes at some later date.

The good Reverend was, of course, duly concerned

[If it can be forgiven me, my concern was primarily with Mrs. King. Mr. Croft or Kraft by this time needed no further assistance from any earthly, spiritual mentor. Mrs. King suffered so much anxiety over his death that I was only too pleased to do everything in my power to acquaint her with as many details as I could learn in the ultimate hope of being able truthfully to assure her that Mr. Kraft had received a decent burial. Unhappily, I was never able to learn what became of his body. I hope that his soul received better care.]

at the news of the sudden and horrendous death of said neighbor and made, if particulars can be excused, several urgent telephone calls from the rectory to ascertain the time and cause of the former's untimely demise and the manner, place, and denomination of burial or interment. God will be pleased to know that the souls of his lambs are in the hands of such a shepherd. This good man also expressed concern about the possible sale of the deceased neighbor's house, there being, as we said, no heir apparent. He, Mr. Perkins, suggested that she might buy it, should it be offered for sale, but she could not see what would be the benefit of owning two houses next to one another when she rarely, if ever, left the one which she had inhabited for two score years and three or four.

The considerate man offered the alternative suggestion that the neighboring house might be razed to afford a more comprehensive view, the lot being worth the same with or without the house. However, on further reflection, the good Reverend, soon to be a doctor, we hope, agreed that the demolishing of a neighbor's house, be he living or dead, might be construed as a sinful act.

[This seems like casuistry to me. As matters unfolded, it would have been far better for all concerned if Mrs. King had followed my real suggestion. However, the reader should not assume that I am in any way enamored, as it were, of views. I only used this argument on Mrs. King in hopes that it might sway her opinion to what I thought was a higher end. I was not altogether unhappy that she rejected the possibility of a better view, since the almighty view seems to me one of the most worldly of vanities and one with which the people of San Francisco are most grievously afflicted. I do not pretend to be a sociologist, but I have noticed a direct relationship between views and suicide in Northern Europe and views and alcoholism in Southern Europe. San Francisco, of course, has an abundance of all three, while its sister city in the southern part of the state is built in a valley and has a lower rate of both, although I suspect that those people who live in the hills around the valley tend to drink and kill themselves more than those who do not. I need only mention that Hollywood is in the hills and not the valley.]

Thus, it was agreed that nature should be allowed to take her course, while we would put our trust in Divine Providence that the house fall into good hands. New neighbors, of course, are never what the old ones were, and it can be hoped only that they (the new) might be as good or better than the old.

APRIL 11, 1960. [*Mrs. King*].

"A Short Sermon on the Text: 'Love Thy Neighbor,'"
by the Rev. Mr. Alfred S. Perkins

[Although the logic of this little tract is fair, the rhetoric is admittedly poor; it has no polish. At the time I wrote it, I was very busy with speaking engagements and had to throw it together during a twenty minute bus ride from a meeting of the Daughters of the American Revolution to the King house. I would have gladly taken it home and reworked it, had not Mrs. King been in great need of consolation in this matter, and, poor as it is, I think it had the desired effect on her troubled spirits. Some of my colleagues suggested that I rewrite the tract before including it in the diaries, but, after careful thought, I decided that this would be a violation of my editorial policy, as established in the Preface, and untrue to Mrs. King, who so scrupulously copied it into her diary. When this was done the sermon was really no longer my property but hers.

The talk I gave before the D.A.R. that day was entitled, "Lenny Bruce: The Immigrant Vocabulary of the 1890's." It has some bearing on the problem of neighbors and can be purchased in mimeographed form from the Secretary for fifty cents in coin. No stamps, please.]

"Often we spend years in close proximity with a fellow human being without ever coming to know and love him as much

*38*

as we are led to believe that God would have us. We must ask ourselves whether we should have made the neighbor dearer to us, whether he should have made us dearer to him, or if it was Divine Providence which made us no dearer to each other than we were. God may have told us to love our neighbors, but He, or more probably His scribe, did not elaborate on this command or explain what was meant by the crucial term 'neighbor.'

"Does 'neighbor' mean the man next door, in the next city, the next state, or the next country? This we do not and cannot know. Did God bid us love those whom we do not know? This we cannot know either, but does not common experience tell us that we do not love those whom we do not know? Nor do we hate them, of course; we are indifferent to them, as they are to us.

"So we must conclude that 'neighbor' does not have a spatial or geographical reference. What other references are possible then? Such terms as temporal, familial, and spiritual come to mind: Temporal, because we love our parents and our children; familial, because we love our brothers and sisters, our aunts and uncles and cousins, both male and female; and spiritual, because we love God and those He has chosen to do His work.

"Therefore, if a man lives next door to us, he is not necessarily a neighbor, since he qualifies for that appellation only in a spatial sense, which has been shown to be inapplicable. Do we know this man or do we only know of him? Such a distinction is not trifling matter, nor is it to be overlooked. We can say that we know ourselves, but we cannot say that we know Paris. We know *of* or *about* Paris. And, if we do not know this man, but only know of him, we cannot love him any more than we can love a foreign city, which we know of or about. Both are geographical phenomena.

"Is this man a member of the family, a blood relation? If he is not, then the familial application of 'neighbor' is not relevant.

"Is this man a member of our church, united with us under one of God's chosen shepherds? If he is not, the spiritual application of 'neighbor' is not relevant.

"It will be said that God would have us love everyone, and we should try to do so, but, indeed, if we loved everyone equally, then those closest to us would be deprived of their fair share of our love, and God would not have us deprive our families of that love which is their due temporally, familially, and spiritually.

"Therefore, it must be concluded that a man who lives in the house next door is not necessarily a neighbor. And, if he is not a neighbor, we need feel no guilt about not loving him, since nowhere does God command that we should love anyone who is not our neighbor, except our enemies. And far be it from me to say that Mr. Croft was an enemy of anyone's"

APRIL 12, 1960. [*Edward King*].


A thing of beauty is a joy forever and beauty is truth, truth beauty. The world will go merrily round and round as long as we have Keatses

> [This poet, John Keats (1795–1821), of course needs no annotation. My favorite of his lines, lines that I used often to quote to the Kings are:
> "And now! ah, I see it—you just now are stooping
> To pick up the keepsake intended for me."]

to note and Skeatses

> [I suppose this is a reference to the Rev. Walter William Skeat (1835–1912), a member of the Anglican clergy and a scholar who is reputed to have done much to further learning in the last century. I understand that this learned man is too worthy to be bandied around in this off-hand, light-hearted manner. However, nowhere is Edward more shamefully abusive and disgusting than he is in this entry.]

to annotate, but beauty of beauties and truth of truths we had our own Chaplin read to us our own sermon on our own Mr. Croft in our own house. Ah, visitations of divine preference, could Solomon have wanted more wives, being offered this instead? And never once did old Alf blush, even after poisoning our neighbor geographical. Perhaps our neighbor died only to provide a suitable subject for a sermon, and men have died for

*41*

less, I guess, and men have died for less. Croft himself would have poisoned himself long ago in happy anticipation of such an elegy. Yea, would have risked eternal Helen D*mnation for P*ss-Pot Perkins' purple passages of pulsating, petulant prose. A life given over to solitude has its rewards: peace, peace and occasional prophecy and, O, bated breath, Perkins perorating before the fireplace, it as cold as he hot with praise for Croft now born aloft, for Kraft now surely quaffed. O, preaching pudendum, souppoisoning parson, bring us yet another draught that we may drink as deep as Socroftes, that we may die as dead a death and live with Croft forever in the classic culminations of such pseudo-Ciceronian slop!

[To the Reader:

For a period of two months, neither Mrs. King nor Edward made any entries into their respective diaries. The reason for this must, I am afraid, remain a matter of conjecture, although both parties give different but, I think, ultimately unacceptable explanations.

Mrs. King, as the reader will soon learn, explains that she felt it necessary to observe a two month period of mourning for the late Mr. Kraft, and in so doing, had to relinquish all pleasure in life. This is not unlike the Lenten practices of the Roman Church, but it is difficult for me to accept her statement as fact, in part because of her scant acquaintance with that man and in part because I had thought and still think that my sermon, brief and unpolished as it is, went no small way in suggesting to Mrs. King that she had no real obligation to the deceased. Only the Roman Church sings services for the dead.

Edward King's explanation, although possibly a true one, certainly does him no credit as a son or a gentleman. That he should hide her diary from his mother, when it was one of her few pleasures in life, is not totally out of line with his indifferent moral character. However, that he should do so for a period of two months is almost beyond my power to believe, even of one such as he.

It might appear that each is, as they say, "covering up" for the other. If this is the case, I can only say that I am frankly at a loss as to which one to believe. The reader must, I think, make his own choice.

A. SYLVESTER PERKINS, D.D.
*St. Moritz, Switzerland*
*October 31, 1964*]

43

JUNE 11, 1960. [*Mrs. King*].


Two whole months have passed by her since she last wrote,
two months dedicated in their sublime entirety to an unofficial
mourning period for the late, lamented Mr. Silas Croft, a
neighbor.

> [Another indication that my sermon did not have its
> desired effect.]

Too long, perhaps, for one not really connected with the family, not really connected with family, not really connected at
all, except in a geographical sense, but then a neighbor of long
standing. Who would have dreamed that death might knock at
a door so near and carry off Mr. Croft to his final reward? Vacant now the body which housed his soul, and vacant, too, the
house which held his body. How strange it is that houses are
resold and bodies, much the nobler work of the two, are left to
perish and decay.

Would she then be any more justified in purchasing his
house, which held his body *and* his soul, than in purchasing
the body which held only his soul? Even if there is little or no
danger that a new soul might decide to move into Mr. Croft's
vacant body? Certainly, a fitting topic for a sermon: "Bodies
for Sale."

> [The strange metaphysics of this entire passage indi-
> cates that Mrs. King had been listening to some of
> the wild ideas of her son. He at one time attempted
> to communicate some of these same ideas to me, but
> I quickly put a stop to any such nonsense as that.

44

Perhaps, I should have been wiser to listen, since it might have thrown some light on the dark surfaces of his mind, making these diaries of greater value to teachers of anthropology and their students. I do, however, remember Edward's mentioning a poet he called Done from whom he read me several passages, unfavorably comparing Lord Tennyson to them. If reference books were available to me here, I would hunt out these lines. The title of the sermon suggested by Mrs. King is, of course, highly unacceptable and for very obvious reasons.]

We must suggest it to the good Reverend, who still persists in suggesting that she buy Mr. Croft's house. No, better she buy his body, except that the good man does not know whatever became of it, while the house is still very much next door. But, perhaps, like Mr. Croft's body, wherever it may be, his house will remain vacant forever and then decay. In this way it would belong to no one but God and be much more like his soul than his body.

Perhaps there is even a heaven for houses, but that seems wrong. Yet, she cannot imagine a heaven without her house.

[The only evidence for this is *John* XIV, 2: "In my Father's house are many mansions." The Revised Standard translation of this passage has "rooms" for "mansions," which makes much better sense.]

It would be like moving to a new apartment. Everything would be strange, very strange. We wonder if the good Reverend has ever thought of that, but then his little cottage is so small.

[The curious reader may be interested to know that I was at this time admirably provided with a house of two bedrooms, one of which was converted into a study and television room. In conversation, Mrs. King had the habit of making unconscious comparisons between her affluence and my modest means. Like moneyed people in general, however, she did not equate wealth with moral superiority.]

He probably would not mind moving away. He has not really lived there very long and, since it belongs to the church properties, it is not even really his. Little wonder that he is so anxious to move others around. But there is a consistency in that, for he encourages people to move into new apartments and to go away to heaven.

A rolling stone gathers no moss and a mossy stone does not roll. Lord Henry and Sunday

[These two characters appeared in a morning radio serial sponsored by the Whitehall Pharmical Company, so I do not think it can properly be designated as a Soap Opera. I have always thought that Sunday was a very charming, original name and wondered why it never gained common currency. The Spanish, of course, use the name Domingo, meaning Sunday, for boys. They even go so far as to call some of themselves Jesus Maria, which sounds more like an oath than a name.]

would never have left Black Swan Hall, even after they found that body in the swimming pool. Sunday, of course, did leave that mining town in Colorado to marry Lord Henry, but, one supposes, he could not very well have gone to Colorado with her instead. It is quite clear that in their case, someone had to move. Hence, Sunday was the rolling stone and Lord Henry the mossy one. Edward, her son, is a mossy stone and so is she.

Reverend Perkins, however, is a rolling stone like Sunday, and Sunday and a reverend go very well together, so she supposes things are as they should be. If Sunday had not married Lord Henry, she might have married the good Reverend, and then they both would have stopped rolling and could have moved into the Croft house.

## JUNE 12, 1960. [*Edward King*].

I couldn't stand it any longer. The day Alfy read his sermon, *Ma* (*man*) *chère* donned a black hat to match her dress and swore to spend all her time in her sitting room, thinking about rotting Mr. Croft. Better had she listened to the charitable words of her Spiritual Mentor, Financial Advisor, and Infanticidal Friend: "Ah, my dear Mrs. King, if God had wanted you to mourn so, He would have taken away someone nearer and dearer to you." Mrs. King, good soul that she naturally is, screams, "My Edward, my poor orphaned boy," and faints dead away into the flagellating arms of Alfred the Great Consoler. Poor darling. Such a poor port in a storm is Perkins. But, she kept her promise and would have very little to do with me and nothing at all to do with Chamber Pot Perkins.

[By this time the reader should be well enough acquainted with Edward's character to be able to appreciate the tedium of my visits alone with him. However, I never varied in my visiting habits but once, when the death of a mail-clubber (see below) called me to Hayward, California.]

Thus, he became my charge for two whole and entire months. Ah, Croft, whatever did I do to you to merit such a foul revenge? What could I do but take revenge myself. On whom? A. S. Perkins Unavengeable? How, be rude to him, cast p*ss in his face shrewishly and give him the advantage of an epic simile to maintain his fame? Never.

What did I do, O, crawl, you foul fiend, stinking end, crawl

*48*

to the table and take that diary out of that poor woman's hands and hide it for two whole months.

[I cannot resist saying once more how appalled I was when I first read this. If Edward had been alive the day after I received his diary, I would have chastised him thoroughly. I have made a comment on his innate thoughtfulness regarding his mother which, after further consideration, should be withdrawn.]

And not another in the house, nothing, nowhere, only toilet paper, and then not to be able to tell Perky to get you another because he would know what had happened to the last one. And he would say nasty things about your boy, your mother-torturing son. No diary, no Perkins, just your black hat and rotting Croft. A fit revenge if not an admirable. Over now.

Couldn't bear it. All's well that ends well, as Marx said, and so Perkins came today with a bouquet of roses for us, sweet man, and told us Mr. Croft's house had been sold, but he didn't know who bought it,

[The real estate people were very uncooperative, when I called, until I identified myself and stated my fears. They had no information available at the time, however.]

Itoldyousoingly (Adverbs of the world, unite!). Fun. New geographical neighbors to die off and mourn over like flies. A family of six could keep us occupied for a year. I hope the soup-bearer doesn't get any ideas. May they all be members of his congregation. That will make nine, including himself.

[For the record, my congregation at this time consisted of no less than 541 active members, 213 inactive members, and 56 postal-clubbers, a plan whereby people moving out of the parish area could, if they chose not to join another congregation, receive our Sunday church services by mail and return their offerings on Monday in the same way. Twice yearly we mailed out a type of C-ration wafer and powdered grape juice, which I understand was used by Army chaplains during World War II. The water used to mix the juice was blessed by extension in accordance with Fiat No. 489 of the Board of Deacons Elect and Reigning.]

JUNE 15, 1960. [*Edward King*].


Tomorrow is F Day.

[As the reader may be aware, this is the second
mysterious allusion to this particular day. Repeated
perusals of the diaries have yielded no light as to its
possible significance. I am forced to conclude that it
is a mythical festivity in which Edward alone partici-
pated. Its meaning has gone to the grave with him,
perhaps not for the worse.

One of my more eclectic colleagues has pointed
out to me that this entry bears a striking resemblance
to the work of that school of poetry which flourished
a few years ago in the North Beach area, which is
within walking distance from the King's neighborhood. That Edward was familiar with this school
must remain conjectural. How he could have known
it is beyond my powers of deduction.

The school of poetry has since ceased to be associated with this area, which has undergone a sort of
urban renewal.]


Would we could ask Mother Perkins to officiate at the Com-
memorative Festivities. How else to bring Religion, pure and
true, into so sanctimonious a ceremony? Did not Clytemnestra
and Orestes have their priest by Agamemnon's bier? "Buy
Agamemnon's Beer. Enjoy one in the bath. See Lycidas

[A character in an early poem by John Milton. In this poem Mr. Milton, in the great tradition of English poetry, attacks the Roman Church.]

floating on his watery beer. Edward King. Yuk. Yuk. Can you guess my secret? Secrete. See Crete, home of Agamemnon's Beer. The Bier that made Mycenae famous." O, fond memories of my father, now ten years gone—but, as they say *in carminibus*, the memories linger on. Yes, the memory of my mother imploring my father, whom she felt did not love us enough, to show that love. "Laius, Laius," she implored, "O, please, Laius." Shades of Oedipus Wrecks, King of Thieves. Pun, pun, pun. See Spot pun. Pun, Spot, pun. Out, out damned Spot. Your puns are ruining the hardwood floors. The pun is the lowest fume of Homer. Creaking Greeks, we are back to the classics. See Cretely.

I, Edward King, have been deliberating whether to write an ode on the memory of my father—he had a very fine one—or on the pun, which by marvelous and significant coincidence begins with the same, exact and identical letter as does "father" in Latin—shades of the triumvirate—where are the bones of Pompey now? Since the latter course is the more fitting, I have decided on it and hence have scrupulously borrowed a line from myself with which to commence. I commence:

> Pun, thou lowest fume of Homer,
> Related to my father, wayward roamer,
> Just like *Pater* of Latinity,
> Some have called you quibble.

Having thus soared to Parnassian Heights, unparalleled in the *historia literaturae,* I will return to prose, since poems are like apples and prose is a rose. Nonsense, I stray: the festivities are yet to be planned.

"Dedication to a Decade of a Dead Dad"

This would be the title of a funeral address if Pious Perkins, the man with the dangling participle between his legs, were to read it, or write it, which, *in absentia sua,* I must write myself:

[What follows is, I am certain, a satire on the tract I read before the Kings. If the satire were not so silly, I would expurgate it as sacrilege. If there are any censors less lenient than I, let them remember that the Satanic voice raised against the Lord is like the praise of Angels in His ears.]

"Friends," saith Alfred Exordiator, "others before us have lost a father and some cannot be said to have ever had one. J.C. had a father. But has anyone ever found a father for God the Father? No, only God the Son has a father, God the Father. Some theologians have made an infamous attempt to say that God the Holy Ghost is the father of God the Father and the Grandfather of God the Son. This is untenable, since God the Grandfather is a dove, and doves do not father Gods or grandfather Sons of Gods who are, in part, men. God the Son gained much prestige by saying, "God is my Father." He would have gained little by saying that his grandfather was a dove. Urchins on the street would have despised him and made sport of such a remark. They would have said, "His grandfather is a bird." Thus, they would not have been saved, although it is doubtful that, in any case, they would have been or were saved. Therefore, I return. Can we, who have never had a father, complain because we have him no longer, when God the Father, who is everything and has everything, does not have a father? Horatio Alger and I say no. If we have a mother or a son, we must rejoice that we once had a father, and we must rejoice that this father gave the mother and the son his name before he was carried away."

Realizing that their father was a prince, or a King, among men, the hitherto as per instructed, rejoicing audience now breaks forth with tears, applause, and acclaim for Perkins Perorator, unsurpassed unraveler of misunderstood mysteries. He concludeth: "Hail, hail. Straight gin will be passed out among you for those of you who have become tense from emotional, intellectual, spiritual, and/or sexual exhaustion and need a massage. All those carrying candles are requested to extinguish them prior to indulging in this fortuitous medicinal exercise. To the memory of one long gone but not long forgotten, hail, hail!" (Exit, pursued by a bear.)

I cannot bear this any longer—Goodbye, Edward, you naughty boy in the Elizabethan sense—until the 17th for a whizz of a journalistic account of the actual, factual, true and real representation of these events as they actually transpired *sub rosa*. But I haven't reached the bottom of the page,

[A page of the handwritten diary does not, of course, correspond to a printed page.]

and I promised myself that I would, each time: 1. So that I cannot be accused by anyone of wasting precious paper needed to feed the poor, starving children in Europe and, 2. so that I will endeavor to expand upon my thoughts, fearing that I am always too brief, too unspecific, too doodle, e doo, dum, dum, la di da, Ah.

JUNE 16, 1960. [*Mrs. King*].


She has discovered, quite by accident, as it were, that her son, while she naps in the afternoon from three to five, has been rummaging around, if a slang phrase may be borrowed, in the attic amongst the old books

[It was said that Lawrence King, an avid collector of first editions and other rare books, had a collection worth in the neighborhood of a quarter of a million dollars. This collection was stored in the attic because Mrs. King feared that the maids, when there were maids in the house, would object to having to dust the old books. The Arson Inspector concluded that the fire probably started in the attic among these books. My pointing out to him that Edward often read there with a candle (see this entry, below) confirmed his suspicions.]

which once belonged to his dead or departed father. Only this very day, awakening from her accustomed sleep at the usual time, did she hear odd and peculiar noises and scufflings in the attic above her bedroom. Fearing that rats might have invaded the house, as the good Reverend Perkins suggested they might,

[There were rats in the house. Various neighbors counted no less than seventy-three leaving the house during the course of the fire. Many must have been overlooked.]

she ran immediately up the last flight of stairs and, much to her surprise and pleasure, found, instead of rats, her son Edward with a candle, once belonging to the chandelier in the foyer, reading in one of the old books his father had had at the university. Imagine her surprise and pleasure, when in the course of this discovery, he addressed his mother in a strange and antiquated foreign tongue.

[Probably Greek, Latin, or Hebrew.]

A new interest for her boy! "Do wonders and blessings ever cease?" she asked herself. How much better for his mind and amusement than reading those awful old magazines in the cellar. When asked how he had come to think of those books, which were moved there after the death or departure of his father,

[A lapse of memory on Mrs. King's part. (See my first note to this entry, above.)]

her son reminded her that today is the tenth anniversary of his death or departure.

Imagine her surprise and chagrin, for she, his wife, had completely and totally forgotten. When one lives alone and secluded from the world, as she does, one must excuse such lapses in memory, for every day is so much like its fellows that it cannot be distinguished from them. However, feeling that she should certainly write something on such an occasion, she turned to her much neglected book of vignettes, at a totally unaccustomed hour, in hopes of being able to jot down a few meaningful thoughts: a small sacrifice to be sure when one considers the excellent example set for her by her son.

As already noted, her husband departed exactly ten years ago this day. She has already expressed her thoughts on the subject of single-handedly raising an orphaned boy—a boy for whom she has had to be both mother and father for the past ten years. Such a task is no easy one, as anyone who has shared it will know, and those who have not may guess. If her years of solitary parenthood have been difficult at times, they have not been without reward at others. One of the greatest rewards was, perhaps, that which she received today, the sight of her son poring over his father's old books, led to do so by the fact that he alone had realized that the anniversary of the departure was at hand. Although his father's books would not have been where they were if his father were still here,

[Another lapse of memory. (See my first and fourth notes, above.)]

he would nevertheless have been proud to find his son in such an attitude. Life, even a secluded one, is not without its rewards and remunerations.

The good Reverend says that he has as yet been unable to learn the names and characters of the person or persons who have purchased the Croft house. He has attempted, purely in the interest of her son and herself, to get in touch with the realtor, but without any success whatsoever.

[Mrs. King was apparently so excited by finding Edward employed at something useful that her memory of past and present events became confused. (See my first, fourth, and fifth notes, above.) The confusion might also be due to the late hour. (See this entry, below.) I had, of course, contacted the realtor immediately upon the sale of the house. That he could not furnish me information concerning the new owners may have had something to do with a professional code.]

He finds this somewhat strange and, for herself, she must admit that suspense is not compatible with age and an uneventful life. Perhap, the good man will come with news tomorrow to alleviate this unpleasant suspense.

It is now long past her usual hour of retirement, and her son has retired long since. She can just see his sweet face tucked up around his neck.

[The metaphor here is somewhat confused. (See above.)]

JUNE 18, 1960. [*Edward King*].


[It has occurred to me that this mythical celebration took place on exactly the same date as the disappearance of Lawrence King. That Edward should even think of this day in terms of celebration is incredible but not inconsistent with his flabby moral character.]

O, woe. The days of wine and roses are over. The last Bacchante is dead or dying upstairs in her bedroom.

[This is strong evidence that Edward is fabricating the story. Mrs. King showed no signs of ill health at this or any other time.]

She had to write a vignette prior to commencement and this the Tenth Anniversary and so tired. She said it was age, but I said Elde

["Elde" probably should be read "Elder" and be followed by a noun. I have not changed it, however, because of my editorial policy.]

was not excluded from the pleasures of my subterranean garden. Are the roses really blown and has the wine turned to vinegar, a panacea for headaches? O, take thou this rose, O rose. No, she who knows snows has blown the rose. So there was no commencement. "I am very tired, Edward, and I am going to bed," said she to me, sitting on the Sacred Stack and admiring the fruits of my endeavors in the world of Art with a glass of Old Massage in one hand and a candle in another. "To bed, to bed, said Sleepy Head. Let's tarry awhile, said Slow. Get off the pot, said Greedy Gut, we'll sup before we go." "Edward," she reprimanded vociferously and stalked upstairs. "Mother," said I in a flood of tears which extinguished my candle and left me in the dark to try to revive my spirits, which had mingled on the magazines with my tears. "M," I said, "is for the million times I've had you. O is for the other things I tried. T is for the breasts at which I suckled and H is for the hell this home's become for me. Put them all together and they spell MOTH, and just give it a candle and it will cremate itself."

I used to go into cocktail lounges when I was a boy. I always sat at the bar, never at a table. Bars are always warm and dark and often red. There is always a lot of nourishment at a bar and you can always see it all from any stool where you sit, leaning against a soft leather pad with your head bent forwards and your feet propped up on the rail. The music is muted and rhythmic, like a heartbeat. I used to sit at the bar with all the old f*rts who lived there, and I knew why they were there and why they didn't leave until it was dark outside.

The policeman who was there all the time because he owned the place, or half of it, used to buy me drinks because I was the son of Lawrence King. When I told him I was Lawrence Prince, he didn't laugh. That's why I turned him in to the ABC.

[This may actually have happened. Mrs. King mentioned to me that there had been some trouble of this nature involving Edward, then sixteen, and a policeman whose name I cannot remember. Edward was not, as I have said, a drinker, so the policeman's offense was probably of another kind. We must remember that a wolf may creep into any flock.]

60

Mother found me the next morning curled up among the magazines and tears with a bottle pressed to my lips. She put me to bed where I stayed all day, missing the visit of Alfred Pee. All joy is gone from the world.

I remember celebrations which somehow seemed to smack more of the *bon vivant*.

["Good living one."]

The Fifth Anniversary should go down in history, a memory of the past Golden Age. It began shortly after dark. All doors double-locked, the windows in the cellar covered with curtains left over from the air raids. The victrola played "Whispering" and "Stormy Weather" and any number of Chicago Blues, collected by my father in Chicago itself.

[Lawrence King was an avid collector of rare recordings. His collection, insured for $100,000.00, was destroyed in the infamous fire. His book collection was not insured, although it was worth considerably more.]

These were the best. Old Massage flowed like champagne in that hotel room across from the White House of 1921.

[This is a nefarious allusion to the odious rumor that President Warren G. Harding did not abide by the Volstead Act.]

Mother wore her wedding gown—why did I burn it—and I wore the suit my father wore when he buried my grandfather. Mother gave a speech on Women's Rights and I moved to p*ss on the Sacred Stack. Thoughts of lingering odors tabled the motion. Mother gave a speech on Civil Rights. The point of the speech was that, if someone could prove that all Negroes were women, all troubles would cease, because the Constitution says only that "men are created equal."

["All men are created equal" does not mean that the government is responsible for maintaining equality after birth. Common sense tells us that grown men vary greatly in appearance, financial status, intelligence, and merit. I assume, therefore, that this statement means only that all men are created, that is conceived, in the same manner and is thus, incidentally, an implicit denial of the Virgin Birth. I do not know if any Congressional committee has investigated the possible anti-Christian interpretation of this passage.]

After I pointed out the effects this interpretation would have on women's rights, the subject was dropped, and we discussed the impeachment proceedings against Andrew Johnson, which Mother thought would make a superb musical comedy: "The Johnson Rag," which we promptly played and danced to wildly and in a wild manner, as she so cleverly phrased and rephrased it.

Fortune cookies were then passed to all.

[Another indication of the falsehood of this and other entries by Edward King. At no time did I ever receive a grocery list from Mrs. King which called for fortune cookies.]

My fortune read: "A voyage by sea or river." After I pulled her out of a consummate hysteria, she read hers: "More effort and fewer tears will help." A short discussion ensued concerning the Sage at the Fortune Cookie Factory. We then spent half an hour contriving fortunes of our very own. I have kept them, dear reader, and present them now for your instruction and delight. The fortunes themselves are, as it were, *utile*, while the cookies, which you must provide yourself, are, you will notice, really quite *dulce:*

1. You probably have cancer.
2. This cookie has been poisoned.
3. Your mother has V.D.
4. Read the 23rd Psalm backwards.
5. The sky is falling. Tell Henny-Penny.
6. Your sister is planning to Mary Martin Luther King. (No relation).
7. Hitler is alive and in this restaurant.
8. 54–40, or fight!
9. Your electric eye needs glasses.
10. It *is* true what they say about Dixie.

This activity was followed by a beauty contest, for which I became a transvestite,

[A member of one sex who dresses in the clothing of the other. This unspeakable practice is very common in San Francisco and sometimes goes unpunished, although it is against the law.]

because of the acute shortage of girls in the cellar at that hour. Mother, Miss Mississippi, won hands down. She was the only judge. And, after reading the Song of Solomon to her *en français,* we retired.

But those days are gone.

JUNE 21, 1960. [*Mrs. King*].


She suspects today that the good Reverend was quite mistaken in regard to the decline of the neighborhood and the surrounding community.

[The reader will see that it was Mrs. King, not I, who was mistaken.]

The new Crofts are moving in today and we can see them from her window, but not them really, their servants. Yes, servants and so many at that. We have already counted six. Two maids, a chauffeur, a young gardener or butler, a housekeeper and her little daughter,

[This description attests to Mrs. King's acute powers of observation, since it is a very accurate depiction of the Robinson family which purchased the old Kraft house. I never had occasion to learn their first names.]

who has probably just gone into service. There have not been so many servants in one house in the neighborhood for thirty-seven years.

[This is probably a specific reference to a particular family. Mrs. King was always very good at remembering dates.]

The new Crofts must be quite wealthy and an established family, perhaps from the Old South. The servants handle the furniture with such great care, almost as if it were their own.

To error, of course, is human. She hopes that the good Reverend is not unhappy to have made such a gross error

[Indeed, I wish I had been in error.]

in regard to the neighborhood and the surrounding community at large, which seems to be, as it were, on the incline rather than the decline. The good Reverend must and will rejoice with us that he has made so grievous an error about the neighborhood and the community at large, as it were.

If she still were in society, as she once was, many years before the ravages of time began to wreck their savage wraths on her furrowing brow, she would have an afternoon soiree to welcome these established people to the neighborhood and the community and the neighborhood at large. They seem, if one may judge from the seeming character of the servants, to be of the same kind and quality of people as Judge Pendleton and his wife, Matilda.

[These are characters in a morning and afternoon radio serial, one major network in the morning and a repeat broadcast on another major network in the afternoon. If I remember correctly, the Pendletons, although wealthy and respected, were often cast in the role of villains.]

It has been twenty-three years since there has been a judge

[This must be a reference to a particular judge. I have not been able to learn his name. (See my third note to this entry, above.)]

in the neighborhood, and twenty-three years is a very long time to be lacking someone of the legal profession, which is little less admirable than the medical.

[This, it must be remembered, is Mrs. King's personal opinion.]

If her son had not decided to live a retired life, she would have had him be a judge or a doctor, preferably the latter, because they are more useful to more of the community at large. Very often, one can assume, those who need the services of the law are not quite proper, while sickness, unlike the law, may strike anyone at anytime and is not an infrequent visitor even among the best of families.

Business, of course, is quite respectable and the Kings were long established in the field of trade,

[Not so well established as Mrs. King might have wished. Lawrence King's father, Alfred, came to California in a covered wagon, a fact about which Mr. King was prone to brag.]

as she has explained before in earlier vignettes. However, to be sure, business is not quite so respectable as a true profession like the law or medicine which requires a good deal more education than a businessman. Some with no education at all have been known to become very wealthy in the commercial area. One has only to recall to mind those shop-keeping railroad people

[Colton, Hopkins, Stanford, and one other, I suppose. Mr. Stanford put his money to a very admirable use as everyone in California is well aware. His university has never been associated with questionable political movements and the like. Henry Huntington, who was also involved with these men, established a library in Southern California which has many fine books. Mrs. King's judgment, therefore, is perhaps a little too harsh.]

as illustrations who have commercialized Nob Hill.

It might have been well that Edward, who has not been well the last few days, had become a doctor in order to prevent this sort of thing from happening. What ever would become of her if something ever became of Edward or him to her?

These are ugly thoughts indeed and cloud the day made brighter by the establishment of the Pendletons in the community and the neighborhood at large. They must not trouble us now, for many and strange are the ways of the Lord, and every cloud has a silver lining, if she may quote from somewhere, they having moved in next door. Mr. Croft must be watching from Heaven with a smile on his face in Heaven where we are certain he has gone.

## JUNE 21, 1960. [*Edward King*].

### Ma Perkins

[This is a reference, not to me, but to Mrs. King. Ma
Perkins was the titular heroine of the radio drama in
which the Pendletons were characters.]

just informed me that Judge Pendleton and his lovely, if
selfish, wife Matilda are moving in next door, i.e. into the venerable old Croft Manse, having cleverly hacked their way
through the Mosses thereof, to paraphrase a venerable old
writer from a Good Family in the East. Ma's been counting
slaves all day and concludes that the Pendletons must be very
well-to-do, to borrow Alfred's favorite phrase, considering the
number and price of slaves these days. Nobody has yet seen
the Pendletons, nor do we expect to until Rastus, Beulah & Co.
have restored the Manse to its antebellum beauty: Shades of
Scarlet O' Letter. Gadzooks, Colonel, an horrendous knock
calls me to the door.

Later.

And, alas, in a very different world. Old A.S.P. has brought
all San Francisco down around my mother's feet. No glorious
earthquake could have done so much to fade that antebellum
flower. It appears that the Pendleton slaves, and not the
Pendletons, have purchased the Croft house. Negroes are in the
neighborhood: Living Here, Real Live Black Negroes, Owning
and not Owned. Shades of Abraham Lincoln.

A.S.P.:

[If my memory serves me correctly, the following scene, which Edward presents in dramatic form, is by and large an accurate representation of what actually occurred at the time. I believe, however, that Mrs. King's reaction was somewhat more vehement than her son, who usually is not given to understatement, presents it.]

O, Mrs. King, I'm so very terribly sorry to bother you at this hour, but I have the most unexpected and, I dare say, unpleasant news to tell you, I . . .

MOTHER: Why, my dear Reverend Perkins, whatever could go wrong today, of all days? The most wonderful thing has happened. Judge Pendleton and his wife are moving in next door.

A.S.P.: No, Mrs. King, I'm most terribly afraid that Judge Pendleton is not moving into the Kraft house.

MOTHER: No? Then perhaps another judge or a doctor. They certainly have a great many servants.

A.S.P.: No, they have no servants.

MOTHER: But, Sir, I have seen them with my own eyes. Six, I believe. Yes, I counted six. A gardener, a . . .

A.S.P.: No, Mrs. King, those are not the servants. Those are the people who have bought the house. Their name is Robinson and they are Negroes.

MOTHER: Negroes?

A.S.P.: Negroes, Mrs. King.

MOTHER: Is Robinson a Negro name, Edward?

EDWARD: Sometimes.

MOTHER: But Edward G. Robinson isn't a Negro.

EDWARD: Edward G. Robinson isn't Edward G. Robinson's name.

A.S.P.: That's quite true, Mrs. King. I believe he's of the Jewish faith, like Mr. Kraft.

MOTHER: Are the Robinsons Jewish?

A.S.P.: No, they're Negroes.

MOTHER: In this neighborhood?

A.S.P.: Yes, Mrs. King, in this neighborhood. I'm so terribly sorry. I told you you should have bought that house. The property values are, well . . .

MOTHER: But the Pendletons, what happened to them? Surely there has been some mistake. Whom do these Robinsons belong to?

A.S.P.: Mrs. King, they have bought the house. It's theirs.

MOTHER: Theirs, Edward.

EDWARD: Mother.

A.S.P.: The executors

[After much diligence I managed to learn the name and address of the executors of the Kraft estate. The following is a copy of the letter which I wrote to them in regard to the sale of the Kraft house. If the letter were not so pertinent to these diaries, modesty would prohibit my including it here:

"Gentlemen:

"In as much as you are by now aware that the house owned by the late Silas Croft of San Francisco has been sold, as per your instructions, I assume, I thought that you might be interested to learn some of the results of that transaction.

"Since I do not feel entitled to appeal to you on the grounds of Christian charity, I can only relate to you objectively some of the results of that sale. For nearly ten years the neighbors of the late Mr. Croft have been under my care and protection. These worthy people, who are of good, old San Francisco stock, have resided in their present dwelling for nearly half a century and have, during that time, seen one of San Francisco's most elegant neighborhoods decline into what can hardly be called little more than a slum.

The recent sale of the Croft house has, as you may be aware, completed this decline.

"This monumental decline has, of course, taken its necessary toll on these worthy people and, coupled with the mysterious disappearance of the head of the family some ten years ago, has perhaps caused their mental faculties to become, if you will excuse the expression, disordered.

"It is as yet too early to fully gauge the effect of the sale on their already impaired mentalities, but I have very little doubt that it may be, as the saying goes, the very straw which breaks the back of the camel. It is, of course, too late to rectify this grievous error beyond mere pecuniary compensation, so I am mentioning it to you only in the hope that you may in future be not only wiser but also more circumspect, and as a means of appeasing what must be a very guilty conscience.

> "Yours respectfully,
> (Signed) *Alfred S. Perkins, Pastor*
> Church of the Respectable Light
> San Francisco, California"

I did not, of course, show this letter to either of the Kings for reasons easily discernible from the text. The remorse of the recipient, who shall remain anonymous in the eyes of man, if not in those of God, is attested to by his failure to respond to this correspondence. What, after all, could he, or they, say?]

in New York have sold it to them. People who have no respect for old San Francisco neighborhoods.

MOTHER: Are these people going to be our neighbors?

A.S.P.: Well, they're moving in next door.

EDWARD: Geographical, so to speak.

MOTHER: God is wreaking his vengeance on us because you and Reverend Perkins did not mourn for Mr. Croft. You should never have poisoned him, Reverend Perkins. Edward was right.

A.S.P.: Really, Mrs. King, I realize you're in a state of extreme anxiety and tension, but please . . .

MOTHER: The Vengeance of God! Whatever must Mr. Croft have told Him about us? Isn't there a law?

A.S.P.: Not any more. I've been to City Hall, and they say that the property values won't drop, which, of course, is a lie.

MOTHER: Whatever will happen to us? You don't suppose they'll want to visit us?

EDWARD: Nobody visits us, Mother.

MOTHER: Reverend Perkins does, but I wish he'd not come to-day.

A.S.P.: I'm sorry, Mrs. King, but I felt that someone had to tell you.

EDWARD: And you're the only one who ever tells us anything.

A.S.P.: Exactly.

EDWARD: Aren't you kind?

MOTHER: And dutiful as well.

A.S.P.: What are you going to do, Mrs. King?

MOTHER: I'm going to my room. You and Edward should pray for guidance.

A.S.P.: I'm afraid I must really be going, trotting off, you know. My sermon, you know.

EDWARD: Good.

MOTHER: Edward and I shall pray alone. I shall pray upstairs and he will pray downstairs. God will surely hear us that way. But do you think they'll harm us?

A.S.P.: Really, Mrs. King, now is the time you should really think about selling, before the market really drops. You still might . . .

EDWARD: Goodbye, Perky. (Exit Mother.) Did you sell the house to them?

A.S.P.: I really must be going, Edward. My sermon, you know and Sunday's getting closer every day.

EDWARD: Aren't you sorry you poisoned Mr. Croft?

A.S.P.: Goodbye, Edward.

EDWARD: Are you going to poison the Robinsons?

"I'm so very awfully glad to have you in the neighborhood, Mrs. Robinson, and I know how busy you've been with moving and all, and I just thought you might like this little tureen of soup to sort of tide you over, as it were. Mr. Kraft, the previous owner of your lovely dwelling, was particularly fond of it. He doted on it until his dying day."

[This, of course, is Edward's little fiction. The Kraft-Soup joke became a standard with him, and I felt that opposing him in it would lend too much dignity to such an absurd assertion.]

JUNE 24, 1960. [*Mrs. King*].


She is, of course, asking for humble guidance from Divine Providence in this, her hour of deep and profound suffering and necessity, when, perhaps, the various pillars of society are falling downward about her aging feet. The dutiful Reverend Perkins informed her in all seriousness that Judge Pendleton and his lovely, if selfish, wife Matilda are not moving into the Croft house. Instead, the house has been purchased by a family of another race, a rare occurrence and one which has never happened in this neighborhood or the surrounding community at large.

The dutiful Reverend has said that no law can stop them and that, indeed, many people, white people at that of the lower sorts, are very anxious to move black people into good neighborhoods in order to make the old aristocracy move into the new apartment buildings which are being built by wealthy New York business people of non-Christian religious views and certain political aliens, the names of which she cannot remember, although they fought in the last war on one side or the other.

[This, of course, is not my exact wording, but a somewhat jumbled paraphrase of what I had thought was a rather clear, if somewhat simplified, explanation of the racial problem in America. I realize that, with the questionable decision of the Supreme Court in 1954, the separate but equal solution to the problem of the races has been destroyed. There are still adherents to this doctrine, and I am not ashamed to admit that I am one of them. The older solution

74

worked admirably well for both races for a long period of time. Any right-thinking person can fully appreciate that Negroes will no more approve of the appearance of a white family in their neighborhood than a white family will appreciate a Negro in theirs. I need hardly point out that the Kings would never have considered moving to the Fillmore district, and I have never heard of a white family in California moving to Mississippi, while there are all too many cases of Mississippi Negro families moving to California.

In time the Supreme Court may have the common sense to reverse their unfortunate decision as they have reversed other decisions in the past. In the meantime, those of us who are in the legal minority must accept the 1954 decision as best we can and do our very best to counteract those alien-inspired movements which are quite literally forcing the races together against their wills and the wishes of the better informed members of both sides. If these movements continue to gain momentum, the day will come when it will be the law that a person of one race must intermarry with a person of another race, intraracial marriage being illegal. This, of course, is extreme. However, like fighting fire with fire, extremes must be met with extremes, and no extreme is too extreme in the defense and protection of True Freedom. As much as I am opposed to the Ku Klux Klan, I can only say that its existence is justified so long as there is an N.A.A.C.P. to thwart it. It is far better to have a cross burned on your lawn than to be murdered by a minority group member in your bed.]

Solitude and isolation, of course, have their rewards, one of which allows time for vignettes and another is that she will not

75

be in any position to decline any invitations which the Robinsons, for this is the name, will offer us to drink tea with them, because we will not answer the door and the good Reverend says he will not bring any because the Robinsons do not belong to his lovely church and neither did Mr. Croft who died.

The good Reverend says that a relative of Mr. Croft's has sold the house to the Robinsons in order to be spiteful to us because neither he nor Edward, her son, mourned for him. The good Reverend is going to write a letter to the relative and reprimand him for his heartfelt

[Mrs. King, no doubt, means "heartless."]

thoughtlessness in regard to the welfare of her son and her.

How can she ever thank that good man for calling her attention the great evil which has uncalled for befallen her and her son? Her house at last is no longer worth anything and the neighborhood has declined. Her son, Edward, may have laughed when the good Reverend called it a black day, but he was kind enough to impress upon her the dire extremity to which this unforeseen, malicious event has brought her and her son. It is now too late to purchase the Croft house, although the good Reverend said that it would be nice if she could buy the house with the Robinsons in it.

[This was, of course, intended as a jest, but Mrs. King seems to have taken it seriously.]

Edward, her son, of course, is too young, as the dutiful Reverend pointed out, to understand the full impact of the horrible thing which has happened to her, as the good Reverend explained.

Nowhere in all the history of numerous radio heroines has

any such event ever occurred or transpired. Although some, I believe, had colored, so they always said, help in the kitchen and with the children, but they did not live next door or in the neighborhood or anywhere in the surrounding community and area, unless it was the Fillmore district which the good Reverend calls Little Nigeria or Subhumania,

[I never made any such statements. These appellatives are surely the inventions of Edward whose facility in coining neologisms far surpassed the ordinary.]

or some such poetic appellative.

The good Reverend, of course, warned us about racial prejudice and said that if white neighbors, like the Pendletons, had moved into the Croft house, and we did not like them, we could not be accused of racial prejudice, but if we do not like the Robinsons, we will be accused of racial prejudice because they belong to a different race. She, of course, will not accuse her son, Edward, of racial prejudice and he has not accused her.

If there is any violence in the neighborhood because of the Robinsons, she is to call

[Mrs. King seems to have forgotten that the telephone had been removed some years before at her own request. Although I disapproved of this action because it only served to increase their isolation, Mrs. King insisted on it because of the number of telephone solicitations which she received even after I had requested that their number not be listed. The final blow, as it were, came when Edward, by means of some sort of telephone contest in which he identified the president on a five-dollar bill, enrolled his mother in a dancing class, having signed some papers which were later sent to him through the mails. Extricating Mrs. King from this contract involved some legal trouble and no little expense to the King estate. If it had not been for a lay acquaintance with the law on my part, the expenses would probably have been much greater.]

the good Reverend who will end it by calling the police.

Edward, who is her son, has said that he does not see why these people are called colored because they are black which, like white, is not a color. The Chinese on Grant are yellow, so they must be colored, because yellow is a color, although Edward says that most of the Chinese he used to see were really very white and much whiter than Edward, who like his father has olive skin, so to speak, but not ripe olive which is black or green olive which is green and therefore colored. Edward has brought her a comical magazine from the last war which has pictures of Germans who are green. However, the good Reverend says that the Robinsons are not Germans and that Germans are not colored, although they are green, which is a color. This is very strange.

Thanks be to God that the good Reverend is coming soon to explain to us in great detail what is going to happen. Perhaps Mr. Robinson is a judge, which will be very nice because she likes the color of his skin which would look very nice in a white collar and a black robe. Certainly, if white is the color of purity and virginity, black is the color of dignity and solemnity, very much befitting the position of a judge who is supposed to be dignified and cannot be expected to have the innocence of a virgin.

[Nonsense. Mr. Robinson is, I learned later, Dr. Robinson, a fact which pleased the Kings very much.

78

Whether or not he is a medical doctor, I cannot say, nor do I know if he is a member in good standing with the AMA (American Medical Association).]

The good Reverend will be very pleased to hear this discovery which will make it very nice to have the Robinsons next door, even if we cannot visit them or they us.

JUNE 29, 1960. [*Edward King*].

Help, I say, help! (Part of speech unknown, e.g. verb, to help: "Help me!" or noun, help: "I need help!") Never, in your hour of need, depend on a grammarian or, for that matter, on a reverend, who may leave you stranded in a ghetto surrounded by murdering Blackamoors and with a widowed mother to protect and one, I stress it, who cannot be made, in one sense, fully aware of the impending dangers of ghetto life. We may, as it were, be murdered in our bed

> ["Beds," presumably, although my editorial policy does not allow me to alter the text.]

or have our eyes plucked out like poor Gloucester, among others, and ask to be led to Seacliff

> [A fashionable, white residential area of San Francisco where it was reputed that the Barber family, a radio fiction, lived. (See this entry, below.)]

by our son, Edgar (a mere matter of phonemes, really), and will we join the Barbers there? No, alas, but dive over, the past tense of which diver is Dover. It is written in the Book of Fate.

Perkins has peregrinated, fled fleeing away,

> [This deserves further explanation, since Mrs. King also refers to my "unexplained" absence from San Francisco for this period of a week or so and the sub-

sequent temporary curtailment of my regular visits to the Kings. I was called to Los Angeles on June 25th for a meeting the nature of which I need not explain as it has no bearing here. However, the meeting was so urgent that I was forced to leave for the airport at a moment's notice. Before departing, however, I both wrote and sent my secretary to the Kings to inform them of my departure. However, since they were not in the habit of receiving mail, they did not look into the mailbox from which I produced my letter for them on my return. My secretary informed me that she received no answer when she knocked at the Kings' door. This, of course, was no surprise to me, since they never opened the door to anyone, having given me a key so that I might let myself in for my visits. I might have given the key to my secretary, but I felt that this would be a betrayal of trust and would, of course, have shocked the Kings greatly, finding a strange person amongst them in their own house. Of course, I was not afraid of the Robinsons, who are probably quite respectable.]

afraid himself of a fatal stabbing in the daylight here in our do-it-yourself Harlem. Negroes, Nubians, Niggers, and Moors have pinned us in. It is like the Alamo (remember it?), and I am like Humphrey Bogart. My stage name is Humphrey Metaphor-Bogart,

[A charming lady whom I met here and whom I permitted to read the diaries informs me that Edward must have meant "simile" for "metaphor," because he said he was *like* Humphrey Bogart. Being in the arts, the lady should, of course, know, although I would not have caught the error myself, being unfamiliar with the technicalities of literature, which some have said is really the province of women, although many men have been great writers.]

of the Back Bay Boston Metaphor-Bogarts, you know, and I am playing that great Indian Chief and Scout (his vocation as a youth, Boy Scout, you know, before Man Chief), that scion of the Hopi aristocracy, Outrageous Arrow.

[A fictitious name, I suppose.]

I am now planted (not actually growing, however) in front of the dining room window behind the sansevieria ("without pipes" for you clods who didn't take part in the French and Indian Wars, which is why they lasted so long, you know, nothing to make peace with) and the sansevieria is planted in front of me, and it, too, is not growing because it is dead (I am not, of course, not yet, anyway) from lack of water of which it may soon get a plentiful supply, since I am not without pipes (for making piece, you know) and have been drinking tea with mother and am just about ready to make teepee here in dining room because spy heap long work and maybe heap, too.

Me Indian, you know, live in Reservation, reserved for me, Outrageous Arrow, and Aging Squaw called Aging Squaw or Chingachgooka

[Another fictitious name.]

who used to be Big Female Sarpent, but Big Female Sarpent expelled from reservation under name of Lilith by missionary who bring Fire Water, cheat Indian of land and wampum.

Now Outrageous Arrow, mother's keeper, spy on Fort Croft where live white man Robinson. Now arrive stage coach in front of Fort Croft, say SEARS,

[I hope that Sears, Roebuck and Company will not be offended by this allusion, considering the source. I also have suffered a number of indignities under Edward's pen. In any event, my apologies to that organization for what, I suppose, is ultimately my responsibility, being in a sense Edward's guardian and executor.]

mean Special Enemies of American Royal Savages, bring big white box containing guns, bullets, fire water. Bring to white man to kill Indian.

Missionary no come. Him fear *white* man Robinson live Fort Croft. Say white man ruin Great Plains, drive Indian away. But missionary no come and Indian still here. Missionary called Chicken Sh*t

[An indignity suffered by me which should be adequate compensation to Sears, Roebuck and Company.]

by Indian. Chicken Sh*t heap big Indian name, but Big Spy heap tired. Try hard, no hate white man and Special Enemies of American Royal Savage, now gone.

Missionary say Indian hate white man, kill him.

[I am not familiar with the missionary work which was done among the Indians during the last century, although I am certain that no sect ever preached hatred to either side. If my American history serves me correctly, I believe I remember that the French Canadians at one time encouraged the French Indians to make war on the English Indians, the English American Indians, that is. This is perhaps what Edward has in mind.]

No can do, man, er . . . a White Man. Maybe Chicken Sh*t want Fort Croft, Alamo, and Great Plains himself. Send note to Aging Squaw, say, Aging Squaw, no give Great Plains and Alamo to missionary Chicken Sh*t when Indian wiped from face of Earth. Say, "Aging Squaw: No give Great Plains to Missionary Chicken Sh*t. Yours sincerely, Outrageous Arrow." Big surprise for Chicken Sh*t, him now no build Happy Hunting Ground here on Earth. Heap big surprise. Him give word of Great Spirit, only get word of greater spirit back. Fair exchange: Word for word. Then Chicken Sh*t can change name to Verb Ate 'Em. Then only eat words.

JULY 1, 1960. [*Mrs. King*].


Once in the lifetime of every woman and she might say man
as well, although this does not have specific application, since
her son, Edward, is still quite young, she begins to grow old.
When this process begins, she cannot say precisely, because a
child is said to grow up rather than old and one never calls
anyone else an old child or an aged child, although the child
does have an annual birthday at the same rate as does an
octogenarian, which she is not, and sometimes on the same
day.

However, she is growing older and, it must be admitted,
aged. She certainly is no longer a child and to think so is only
humorous, although her son, so beloved and so loving, is wont
to address her as his dear child, saying that the child is the father of the man or woman, as the case may be, which is a piece
of philosophy which he has learned from his father's old books.

Radio heroines, of course, like Miss Trent, managed to remain thirty-five for many years which was, to be sure, the
clever ruse of someone and Edward has told her of another
famous character named Punsa Day-Leon

[Probably Ponce de Leon, the Spanish explorer who,
refusing to place his faith in Eternal Life, sought
rather to live forever instead.]

who discovered the fountain of youth in Florida, which she
understands has more mosquitoes and other vermin than her
beloved San Francisco, which has fog and those strange people
next door who are surely not neighbors. Edward, her son, has

said that he would rather die tomorrow in San Francisco than live forever in Florida which is a great relief to her since neither he nor she ever leave the house, a necessary step, one might assume, in going to Florida to live forever with the Day-Leons. Nor does she believe that little jest that Miss Trent spent the last war in Germany having Jewish people transplanted into her by German doctors

[This is a reference to the atrocious rumors which the Communists started about German medical practices during World War II. One can only wish that the Russians had not practiced what they falsely preached against. I refer to the post-war Russian experiments on helpless dogs.]

who ought to have been caring for the sick rather than curing the aged and no one can say that thirty-five is old since Miss Trent, of course, began life at that age.

Ah, we stray and stray, the symptoms of an aging mind, as the good Reverend says, and the pains of age creep into her, bringing thoughts of death and destruction or cremation, which the good Reverend suggests, because it is more aristocratic than being buried in the ground.

[I merely suggested cremation as a possible method of interment because it is more economical in the long run. The Kings, of course, could have afforded to be buried in any manner they chose, but it seems a shame to waste good land on the dead when a simple urn will hold the remains just as well. All members of my church signed a pledge that they would be cremated after I had explained to them the vanities of cemeteries *per se*.]

86

Edward, of course, is not going to die tomorrow, as he has promised, and he will not go to Florida and stay with the Day-Leons whom we do not know. But what will happen to him when she is gone? Even if her ashes are on top of the mantle-piece? Edward would not want to stay alone with her ashes and no one to talk with and the good Reverend will not come to live with him because, alas, Edward says that that would drive him to distraction and away from the house, and alcohol massages will not keep her alive forever, although Edward says that alcohol is used to preserve things.

Dear Stella Dallas was a widow and had a daughter Lolly like her son Edward, and Lolly was to be taken care of by her husband, but Edward would have no one after poor Stella died. Many hours have been spent discussing this terrible and plaguing question with the good Reverend who, good and kind as he is and might be, cannot offer her any suggestions which can really soothe her heart which aches remorselessly over the problems, as presented.

[It was my suggestion that, in the event of Mrs. King's death, Edward should be placed in a private institution where he would be free to live in exactly the same manner he had grown accustomed to at home. I could not, of course, give Edward the care he needed myself, if he were to live in the house by himself. The two of them took care of each other when I was not present, but I seriously doubt if either could have cared for himself alone.]

It is perhaps wisest to leave these problems for another day, a clearer mind, and the presence of the good Reverend, who has stayed away trying to learn about the Robinsons who live in the neighborhood. If Mr. Croft had not died, he might have come to live here after she died, although he did die first, which is somewhat of a blessing in disguise.

[Mrs. King does not mean that she is actually glad of Mr. Kraft's death but that it was better for Edward that he died rather than she. I do not believe that this can be called "bargaining with God."]

Edward, her son, liked Mr. Croft, saying he would give fifty Reverends for one Mr. Croft, although there is not one left, and we rarely, if ever, saw him except on the day he died and, they say, fell off his front porch and screamed.

These meditations on death and Edward should be put aside.

[Nothing I could do or say would comfort Mrs. King in this matter. In conversation, I usually tried to avoid the subject as best I could, since it caused her so much anxiety. She *would* bring it up, however.]

Tears begin to run forth from her tired eye, and, of course, other preparations have to be made for death. For many years, she has promised herself to organize and edit her several volumes of vignettes,

[Whether or not she ever began this project cannot be ascertained, since these volumes, which would have made very interesting reading, were destroyed in the fire.]

which is perhaps the most fitting task for age, since the inspirations of more youthful years may weaken while the wisdom of age may help to check the various rashnesses of more youthful writing and thinking. Man, or woman, as the case may be, is like a clock which runs too fast at first and too slow at last, but all considered, as it were, arrives at the proper hour in the end. Hence, I suppose, the phrase: The Hour Has Come.

Additional vignettes, of course, may be forthcoming because of the Robinsons, who are new problems

[One cannot help speculating that Mrs. King's last days would have been a great deal happier if the Robinsons had had the courtesy to wait a few months before moving into the neighborhood.]

whom she must discuss with Edward and the good Reverend, for, as the saying goes, two heads are better than one.

If only the good Reverend would come soon. Life passes quickly and the problems are many: Edward, death, and the Robinsons.

So she must break her faithful promise, which unfortunately she has many times broken before, to add a new vignette daily to her collection.

[This admission that she is unable to fulfill her promise to herself is probably the first sign that age really was overtaking her, no matter how much she mentioned it herself. To the end, however, she remained in perfect physical health.]

If anyone ever cares enough to publish them, she hopes that they will forgive her this promise, which she can no longer keep for a good reason.

JULY 2, 1960. [*Mrs. King*].


The unfortunate and unexplained absence of the good Reverend

[See my third note to Edward's entry of June 29th, below.]

has driven her back to her little volume of vignettes to add yet another vignette and commune with herself long before she had intended to do so. However, she did have time to go through some of her earlier volumes, which do not, on second thought, seem to need as much revision and editing as she had previously thought, not an unpleasing thought, considering the number and length of these volumes.

However, in going over her old papers, she did run across her Last Will and Testament, which was drawn up not long after the mysterious death and/or disappearance of her son's father and husband. In her last vignette, it will be remembered, she analyzed or attacked the various problems which would arise in the event of her unexpected death or demise. Happily, there is one benefit accruing to such an event which does not fail to please her, that is that the entire estate will go to her son, Edward, which will go a very long way in helping to protect him from the world which has more or less been rejected by both him and her.

In the event, however, that her beloved son, Edward, should precede her in death or die at the same time, the bulk of the estate will go to the good and deserving Reverend's church. She, however, has had some second thoughts on this stipulation. The Word of God certainly should be spread, but it does not seem to me

> [Perhaps Mrs. King's only use of the first person in the course of her entire diary, or at least that part of it which we are fortunate enough to possess.]

that doing so should cost a great deal of money. Reverend Perkins has explained to her on occasion that the Catholic Church is the most wicked of all Christian churches and more wicked than some pagan religions. Her son, Edward, has explained to her that it is also the richest church. Certainly, this proves that money is actually the root of all evil with regard to religion,

> [Money may be the root of all evil, but in order to look at the problem full in the face, we must examine the plant, as it were, as a whole. If the plant of which money is the root is a tomato, then the tomato stems, leaves and fruit are evil, of course. If, however, the plant is a radish, the evil or worthless part of the plant may be cut away, leaving only the money.]

and she believes that the Good Lord has even made this point himself in the Bible, for which reason the Catholics do not pay much attention to it. She, of course, has no idea as to the exact financial state of the Catholic Church, but her estate, the good Reverend has said, is worth more than ten millions, which, of course, is very little money now that the Democrats have been in power since Roosevelt and after that wonderful, old General, who, try as he might, could not undo the damage done to the dollar by the Democrats who gave all the gold in Fort Knox to foreigners in order to have a war with Japan. The good Reverend has even said that many right-thinking Southerners who have traditionally been Democrats have decided that they were wrong and have become Republicans because Lincoln freed the slaves and Roosevelt tried to get them jobs.

Therefore, to make the good Reverend's lovely church rich, must also make it evil, an event which could not but displease him and do him a grave disservice. It must be stopped and so, after a lengthy discussion with her son, Edward, it has been decided that the King estate should be entailed to the University of Southern California, once attended by his beloved father.

[I had thought to keep this matter entirely out of this publication. However, since Mrs. King brings it up and it is alluded to in several other entries, I cannot by-pass it, as I planned, for fear that my enemies, namely the press, will construe my silence as a tacit admission of guilt.

One year after the disappearance of Mr. King, his wife made a will, witnessed by me and duly filed, which, in the event that Edward preceded or accompanied her in death, left most of her fortune to my church and named me executor with the express intention that the dispersal of funds be left entirely to my own discretion.

At the time of the fire, I thought this to be the only will in existence. However, when it was published that the King estate was to be settled, one Mr. Bryan Goldman presented to the court a second will which bore the same date as this entry. (Mr. Goldman had acted as attorney for Mr. King on several occasions prior to his disappearance.) He said the new will, unwitnessed as it was, was received by him in the mail, and he showed an envelope addressed to him in Mrs. King's handwriting and postmarked the day after this entry.

I pointed out to the court that the Kings never left the house and, therefore, could not have mailed the letter. The court, however, decided in favor of Mr. Goldman, who is, I believe, the same Bryan Goldman who was prosecuted on a morals charge in Salinas, California in 1928 or 1929. (That he was innocent in the eyes of that particular court does not, of course, mean that he was innocent in the eyes of Higher Powers.)

The Goldman will left all of the King estate to the University of Southern California in Los Angeles, which Lawrence King attended for two years. This university, now well-established and well-endowed, was once a Methodist school.

The court said that, unless I could prove Mrs. King was *non compos mentis* at the time the Goldman will was written, that will would supersede the earlier one. By this time, of course, the university had hired Mr. Goldman at a handsome fee to protect what they erroneously believed to be their interests, and one newspaper vulgarly said that the case was "cut and dried" in their favor.

Since I knew Mrs. King's true feelings in this matter as well as the evil influence which had acted upon her to make her change her mind, I had no choice but to present these diaries to the court. After the court had declared the Goldman will null and void, I immediately started proceedings against the newspapers, which had done everything in their power to influence the judge against me. Three of the articles on which I based my case follow:

1. Caption: "Rev. Perkins Protests New Will." San Francisco, Sept. 18. The questionable Reverend Alfred S. Perkins of the Church of the Respectable Light today told the court that he had evidence

which would "incontrovertibly decide the court" in his favor. The much disputed King millions trial is now in its third day.

2. Caption: "Judas' Kiss." San Francisco, Sept. 21. Today, the so-called Reverend Perkins presented two diaries to the court as evidence in the hotly disputed King Millions Case. Perkins, who was not available for comment, left the court room with a triumphant smile after the court was dismissed to allow Judge Dawson time to examine the journals.

A secretary at the Church of the Respectable Light, over which Perkins presides, said that the diaries belonged to the late Josephine and Edward King who died here in a fire last April

3. (The following is from an editorial column.) Caption: "Thirty Pieces of Silver." Yesterday, as all the world knows, Judge Dawson, bettering his habitual judicial frown, awarded all eleven of the King millions to the Church of the Respectable Light which, on inquiry, we have found to be the corporate name of none other than the Reverend Alfred Sylvester Perkins himself. We could not learn if the Rev is going to use some of his new money to have *Non Compos Mentis* inscribed on the tombstones of his late friends, but it somehow has a more appropriate ring than the usual Requiescat in Pace.

We had the pleasure of meeting the Rev. Mr. last night in the Tonga Room of the Fairmont where he was celebrating with a few friends, one of whom, because of her English accent, we mistook for Diana Dors. We later learned that she's the secretary over there at the Respectable Light where she must add a few candle-power herself.

When asked about his future plans, the Rev said that, and here we'll have to quote, "atheism or any other foreign religion will never triumph in this country."

Make any sense? No, but somehow appropriate.

The court said that "questionable" (see Exhibit 1) was not a libelous term because of some artificial technicality regarding the school of religion which I attended. As far as I can see, this is just another attack by the courts on organized religion in this country.

The judge said that because I had won the case, he did not see how the newspapers had biased the court against me. When I pressed Exhibit 3, the judge said that this article had appeared after the decision was made and could have had no bearing on it. He did admit, however, that it was in bad taste and told me, of all people, to try to forgive those who had trespassed against me. I, however, do not need lessons in religion from any judge.

This, along with being thrown out of court, has led me to believe that there is actually a conspiracy between the courts and the newspapers against organized religion. My finding that this same judge, who shall not be named, has a brother-in-law who is an editor for the same paper that printed "Thirty Pieces of Silver" has confirmed my suspicions. Something should be done about this.]

The good Reverend has said that education is a very good thing, although she has had all too little of the formal kind herself, and that the University of Southern California, although unfortunately it is not in San Francisco, is one of the few large universities left which does not breed and foster the creed of Roosevelt or other alien credos and beliefs which want to destroy the government of the United States like the

Supreme Court. There are many fraternities there, which is the reason for this, and brotherhood is also a very good thing. Therefore, with the help of her son, she has drawn up another and amended will and testament, but her son, for unexplained reasons, has said that we must not tell this little secret to the good Reverend for whom we are saving it as a nice surprise.

Edward is now looking for the address of his father's old lawyer who will keep the new will and the surprise.

No, no, and no again, we must object, heartily and strongly with vehemence. It cannot be. Why had this not occurred to her before? Why? It is not right and cannot be done, never, never. Edward cannot and must not and will not leave this house. But he says he will. He will leave this house, and he may not find his way back, leaving her alone forever with the Robinsons who are blacks, and the good Reverend has gone and may be dead without his surprise. He says he has seen it

[The mailbox, presumably.]

from the window and will go late at night when it is dark while I watch. He will come back. He will come back. He will tie a cord to his wrist and she will hold the ball of cord and he will come back on the cord which she will hold. He will follow the cord back to her and the house which he will never leave again. It must be done and Edward will place a note in the letter which will say we do not want the lawyer to come and see us or the good Reverend and that he is only to keep the will and tell the university to wait for us to die. But she must say nothing to the good Reverend who has not come for a long time, although Edward has said that he has not deserted her.

JULY 16, 1960. [*Edward King*].


MacArthur and Jesus Christ got together and issued a joint statement: I shall return.

[Most will agree that the pairing of these two names is in almost as poor taste as Edward's abuse of both. General Douglas MacArthur, whom I assume Edward means here, great as he was, was not a Divinity. The General's statement concerning his return was made, I believe, in regard to the Philippine Islands during World War II (more astute students of history may verify this, if they choose) and not in reference to a Second Coming as Edward implies.

Personally, I number myself high among the General's many admirers, and I have never ceased to be appalled that he was removed from his command at a time when his country needed him most. The wisdom of this foolish decision can easily be ascertained by casting a glance at the Chinese mainland, which now abounds with Red Chinese, and at the tiny island of Formosa, which harbors the last of the Yellow Chinese.

It has been my opinion for some time, and I do not think it out of place to mention it here, that strong measures should be taken to prevent the televising of old World War II films which are sympathetic with the mainland Chinese, unless it is made quite clear that the sympathetic mainland Chinese of that period now dwell on Formosa, a fact which all too many of us are only too willing to overlook when the question of recognizing Red China is discussed.]

About MacArthur, we don't know yet, but there are some of us who hope he is lying. About J.C. we're not sure. Much of the world is positive he came and went once and is expected again. Others, however, don't believe he came in the first place or, if he did, that he was somebody else by the same name and hence cannot return, having, as it were, never turned in the first place.

[This is a reference to the people of Jewish faith, who mistakenly believe that Jesus of Nazareth was not the Messiah Himself but merely one of a long line of minor prophets. This erroneous belief probably stems from the ill treatment Christ received at their hands while he was on earth. I doubt very much that Edward got this idea from his mother as he asserts below.]

(I stole this thought from my mothah.) And now our very own portable salvation machine, very much impressed by the efficacy and symbolism of a triumvirate, has also said, "I shall return," after, mind you, he had already returned. Such courage, such faith.

Last week, after an absence of G*d knows how long, Sylvester Salvation flounces up the walk, as far from the Croft-Robinson dwelling as possible, and drops this letter in the mailbox,

[This is one of Edward's outrageous fabrications. While editing his diary, I have been living in perpetual fear that I will overlook one of these falsifications, because they are legion, and thus misguide and bewilder the reader. If the reader is ever in doubt

98

about Edward's veracity, it will be expedient, if not
charitable, for him to assume that Edward has strayed
from the literal truth.]

waits for a minute, and then lets himself in as if he had just left
us yesterday. My po' mothah, hearing the door, flies down the
stairs like the Kittyhawk and says, "Dearest, dearest Reverend,
we had thought you had deserted and abandoned us forever."
    "Dearest lady," *inquit,*

[A Latin form which Edward has included to demon-
strate his erudition.]

"didn't you get the note I sent over *via*

[Although I do not remember my conversation ver-
batim, I am positive that Edward is mistaken about
this, and that it is merely another one of *his* Latinisms,
thrown in for the sake of appearing learned. It is not
my nature to use Latin in conversation for several
reasons:
    Firstly, it is the official language of the Roman
Catholic Church and, secondly, it sounds, I think,
rather pompous and affected.]

(he really said *via*) my secretary? It should be in the mailbox
still."
    And surprise! It was! Surprise, surprise! And he was kind
enough to get the note and read it to us and, after he left us, I
got it and now I will copy it herein for my own edification:

"Dearest Mrs. King,
    "A matter of the utmost importance, I believe, has called me
away unexpectedly. It is imperative that I take the next air-
plane flight to Los Angeles, so, lamentably, it is quite impos-

sible that I reach you before departing. I can only offer you my most profound apologies for thus inconveniencing you, but I know you are in good hands [sic]

[Edward's own addition.]

and that the larder, if you will be kind enough to permit a colloquialism, is well stocked.

"Should any unforeseen circumstances arise during my absence, I suggest you contact my secretary, Miss Thorpe, at the church. I have instructed her to be of any service to you, if need be. I shall, of course, return as soon as possible.

"[Signed] *Reverend A. S. Perkins*
Reverend A. S. Perkins
Church of the Respectable Light
San Francisco, California"

How very thoughtful of him to think of us. My whole attitude toward this paragon has changed, and so I could not but ask him what noble pursuit he had been engaged in in our sister city to the south (his phrase). Modest man that he is, I virtually had to drag it out of him by force.

[On the whole, I remember Edward's being very unpleasant on this particular day. My errand in Los Angeles was of no concern or interest to the Kings, and so I did not press its content on them. Edward, however, showed all the curiosity of an adolescent, and so I was forced to explain something of the nature of the trip to satisfy his annoying inquisitiveness.]

It would seem that he and some other noteworthy citizens have banded together to form some sort of council which will, among other things, make the world safe for democracy. He denied, of course, planning to re-stage World War I, but one never knows about him since he's so terrifically modest. He may even be planning World War III to make the world safe for the world.

And so once again he reflounced into our dusty domain, bringing with him the fresh, vibrant air of the outside world and the democracy which pulsates around us. Once again was the breath of life rebreathed into us, while we, reinflated, once again began to hum sympathetically like something set near a dynamo of modest, if infinite, magnitude.

And, as he left with long and cumbersome grocery list in hand, I, reinspired, asked if he would be my partner in an archery shop called The Outrageous Fortune.

[This remark was, and still is, lost on me.]

As he was just about to recoup with one of his witty, incomparably clever retorts from the walk, the loveliest of the Robinson girls gave him a good day. "Not so good," said he, "I like the climate better in Los Angeles." Too bad they're not his dying words, so indicative, so quotable, so memorable.

# JULY 16, 1960. [*Mrs. King*].

For herself, of course, she was not particularly disturbed by the mysterious and lamentable disappearance of the good Reverend, but her son was so troubled for her sake and his own, that the pleasing reappearance of the Reverend contributed much to their mutual joy and satisfaction.

We believe that mysteries are very healthy and contribute much to the interest of life, but all in all it is much more pleasant to have them on the radio than in one's own household. Of course, the good Reverend did not plan this mystery for her and her son but sent the key to the mystery to them before the mystery had even begun which, if she had received it, would have prevented the suspense necessary in order to have a mystery.

All things, as usual, have worked out for the best and now the mystery is over and the good Reverend has returned from an errand of mercy in order to perform many others here in his own city and hers and Edward's.

Nothing, apparently, can be done about the Robinsons who live next door, and she believes that the good Reverend has done everything in his power to bring back Mr. Croft who screamed or some other member of his family to which the house may still belong.

[Mrs. King had apparently forgotten that the house had been sold to, and not rented by, the Robinson family.]

Edward, of course, will not marry any or all of the Robinson daughters because he never leaves the house and has sworn never to marry in order that he may take care of her and she of him. Second sons or daughters may marry whom and when they please, but Edward realizes that as an only son he has a responsibility to his parents or parent, as the case may be. Sunday and Lolly,

[The daughter of Stella Dallas, I presume.]

of course, married, and Lolly always took very good care of her mother because her husband was very wealthy and Stella could take care of herself. Sunday was, no doubt, an orphan, or she may have mailed monthly checks to her mother who, if alive, no doubt lived in that mining town in Colorado which Sunday left. We cannot blame her for leaving such a place, especially if she did not leave a lonely mother there to perish in the cold winters with which Edward says Colorado is very often afflicted. Mary Noble was always married to her husband and did not mind it at all.

The good Reverend has written her such a lovely note so full of kindnesses about his departure that she can only be very sorry that she did not receive it and copy it into her volume of unpublished vignettes. It is certainly a much better letter than any of those written by that servant girl who married her master after a very sordid affair of the type which one used to read about in the newspapers.

[This may be a reference to a novel which Edward may have read aloud to his mother. Those interested in such things may be able to identify it, if they choose, from the facts which are presented here by Mrs. King. I have never been much given to novel reading myself, since I prefer the truth to the imaginative workings of a mind that may very well be unhealthy. I find the whole idea of making up little stories rather juvenile, and for that reason I cannot identify this particular reference for the reader.]

Letters, generally, are such a pleasure to read and write, but Edward says that all her letters were written by a man of all things. Nothing of this nature ever happened on the radio, although there was a second Mrs. Burton, which shows that some are better left unmarried in the first place.

If Edward insists on reading to her on occasion, there are a number of books, which belonged to his late father, which are surely more edifying and truthful than the letters of a servant girl written by a man.

The good Reverend, who has promised never to leave again without saying goodbye, has also promised to bring some books which Edward will read to her and which will edify both him and her.

[Unfortunately, my life was so full at this time that I completely forgot this little promise which Mrs. King says I made her. If the house had not contained so many books, I might have remembered, but, as it was, the Kings were really quite adequately provided with reading material. Not having made a survey of the library myself, I cannot, however, make an estimate regarding the types of books contained in it. The late Mr. King, as I may have mentioned before, was, I believe, given to strange tastes in reading matter. It would, perhaps, have been better had I left some books of my own choosing. In any event, this might have provided some grounds for conversation with Edward, to whom it was always rather difficult to speak.]

She cannot very well read to herself since old age is playing havoc with her old eyes, and she must spare them as best she can for her little volumes, which even now begin to hurt after so little strain. She well remembers when she could write for four or five hours at one sitting without being troubled by her eyes failing her as they are now wont to do. Perhaps, in future, even less frequent entries will be necessary, giving her even more time to think, which may in the long run be well because a concise thought will, of course, require less time and effort to rewrite and reconsider when the time comes for such operations.

Today's special thankfulness goes to the good Reverend for his lovely letter and his various and sundry kindnesses and considerations.

[Mrs. King was always very receptive of any kindness or consideration which I had occasion to offer her.]

JULY 20, 1960. [*Edward King*].


I was stranded with that son of a b*tch for two hours, and so I said to him in all seriousness—and I am capable of it:

"The world is a very funny place." And he said, "which is a prelude (he uses very fine language now, because he has become very sophisticated—a first rate, sophisticated Okie) to what?"

[If by this Edward means that my place of birth was the state of Oklahoma, I must assure the reader that it was not. I was both born and raised in Marietta, Ohio.]

"Nobody ever meets any really happy people anymore,

[The reader will, of course, realize that Edward had not met anyone for at least ten years and thus is hardly qualified to make such a sweeping generalization as this.]

and if you do, the happy people are so quiet that you think they're stupid."

"Which is a prelude to what?" repeated the one who lectures and does not like to be lectured to.

"Right now my mother is upstairs praying . . ."

"A worthwhile endeavor to be sure, but I had wished to see her while I was here." (She'd been there praying all day and wouldn't even come down to greet SOBASP.)

"Do you know *Genesis?*" I said.

"Very nearly by heart, but do you think your mother will come down to see me?"

"Where the world turns white with light?"

"That's not exactly how it happens."

"My mother thinks it is, and she's upstairs now praying . . ."

"Yes, you told me that already."

"Shut up. Praying that the Robinsons will turn white like the world did with light in *Genesis*. Yes, . . . ."

[I firmly believe that the Lord has intervened and taken into His own hands some of the editing which I forebore doing because of my policy.

Not long ago I boarded a train for Baden-Baden. About 6:00 P.M., or 1800 hours, as they say here, I left my compartment with my briefcase in it to go to the dining car for supper or, more properly, *Abendessen*, taking with me Mrs. King's entry of July 16th and, inadvertently, the first page of Edward's entry of July 20th, to which this note is appended, in hopes that I might have a few spare minutes during supper to prepare a footnote or two.

When I returned to my compartment, the briefcase was missing and with it those parts of the diaries which I was then in the process of preparing for publication. I consider it very fortunate that the whole of the remainder of the diaries was not in the briefcase, but only the remainder of Edward's entry of July 20th and those entries up to but not including Edward's entry of December 8th. The final entries, along with those I had already prepared, were in my luggage, which I had had the foresight to check at the station.

It might be said that I was foolish to leave my briefcase unguarded in an empty compartment, but I have a naturally beneficent attitude toward my fellow man and had no more thought that someone might take my briefcase than I would think of taking someone else's myself. Happily, however, there was nothing of value in the case, except, of course, the diaries, since I had had the foresight to secure my passport, traveler's checks, and bank drafts in a money belt.

Fortunately, I had perused the stolen entries several times and, therefore, can give the reader an adequate, if brief, synopsis of what they contained: Edward continued to be as obscene and abusive as ever, although he grew in his own strange way a bit more philosophical both in his entries and in his conversations with me. His mother, on the other hand, gradually became even more of a recluse. She often refused to come downstairs during my visits and, according to Edward, spent less time with him than she had been previously accustomed to. It does not appear that she was more than usually occupied with her diary, since her entries were no more frequent and no longer than they had been for some months previous. During this time, however, she did develop what I believe is called an obsession. She somehow came to believe that Edward had fallen in love, as it were, with one of the Robinson girls, a fact which is belied by Edward in his diary and in his conversation with me. The Robinsons, of course, were sometimes discussed by us but in a very general way. I doubt if Edward even knew of any of them by their first names, since he would have had no way of learning them, except from me and I did not know them myself. Mrs. King's strange idea must be regarded as a figment of her imagination, which was perhaps overworked by the strain of having new neighbors.]

DECEMBER 8, 1960. [*Edward King*].

What a stupid day to paint a house. What a dumb day. What an ignorant day. What a day ignorant of sunshine. What a figure of speech. A poem. Haiku. I like Haiku. E.g., it's foggy. Drip, drip, fog. Drip, drip, paint. Our house is painted with fog while their house is *being* painted with paint. The Festering Lily said those blacks don't have a brain in their head (if one thinks about it, it makes sense—six heads, six brains, no communal head, no communal brain) to be painting on a day like this. "But, Fester," said I, "they're not painting. They're *having* it painted white by white painters."

"That's an arrangement you'd never see down in Goon Corners

[This fictitious place is a creation of Edward's imagination.]

where I was born," said he, smelling worse than weeds.

"Yes, I know," I said, "in Goon Corners them blacks paint the white houses black."

"No, the blacks paint the white houses white."

That, of course, is a redundancy or a waste of paint or, on second thought, a lead-in for a few nasty comments on the President, Dwightie Eisenhauer, which I put a stop to by walking out of the room.

And that's Emily,

[Edward seems to have invented this name for one of the Robinson family.]

my Black Orchid, there through the curtains, watching the white painters paint the house white. There used to be a hedge where Emily is standing, but before the painters came, all the hedges went, and Mother went with the hedges because Mr. and Mrs. Robinson could look into her bedroom (she thought) from their bedroom. I don't know where the hedges went, but she went to the back bedroom and to our own hedges, along with the birds who used to live in Mr. Croft's hedges.

But Emily is better than a hedge, for she is an Orchid and I'm Luther Burbank.

[A horticulturist and atheist who lived in Santa Rosa, California, which is about fifty miles north of San Francisco.]

I'm growing an Orchid in the fog outside and a Festering Lily in the dust inside. The Orchid is female, and the Lily is—guess who—Lily White ASP from Goon Corners. Sacred White Alfred Sylvester Perkins. SWASP, an anagram: WASPS =White Anglo-Saxon Protestant SH*THEAD.

"You'd think those Robinsons thought they were San Francisco socialites, the way they're a-gussying up the old Kraft place," said he.

[I doubt that I have ever used the word "gussy" ever in my entire life, which suggests the dialogue attributed to me in this entry is also fictitious as a whole. The Robinsons, however, did spend a great deal of time and, I dare say, money remodeling the old Kraft place. It subsequently lost much of its original rustic charm, at least for me.]

And the carpenters came and went.
"I wonder what gosh offal color they're going to paint it."

And the white painters came with white paint and painted it white. White paint to house my Black Orchid.

"They must really be getting themselves head over heels in debt," said Lily. And the mason came and went.

D*mnation, she's looking at me.

[This allusion as well as the one above suggests that Edward was watching the Robinsons through the dining room window which faced their house. I suppose he had little else to do, but the idea of eaves-dropping strikes me as repulsive.]

No, she's only looking at our house, commenting, I suppose, that it could use a coat of paint. Oh, my flower, don't you know, beauty is only skin deep. It's the white heart inside that really counts. I've heard the word.

And the other word: When the summer months come, saith Lily White,

[Disregard the remainder of this entry entirely.]

they'll all be on the front porch eating watermelon and f*cking each other like mad, son and daughter . . . father, mother . . . brother, mother, . . . father, daughter, hadn't oughter. But not my Orchid, my Emily. No, not she. Besides, you dumb sh*t, Frisco, as you used to call it, you clod, doesn't even *have* any summer months.

DECEMBER 10, 1960. [*Mrs. King*].


We do not and cannot remember anyone by the name of Emily

[It would seem that Edward may have told Mrs. King about his hypothetical Emily.]

in radio fame, and certainly no heroine by that name, which, after careful consideration, seems to be the kind of name by which one might call a servant. Josephine is, of course, the name of an empress

[Probably the wife of Napoleon I of France (1769–1821).]

who was very beautiful, and Edward is the name of a number of the kings of England, including the last one, who married someone by the name of Wally,

[Wallis Simpson, who married Edward VIII and scandalized the world. (Mrs. King, no doubt, means the last king named Edward, since the last king was George VI, the brother of Edward VIII and father of Elizabeth II. Philip is Prince Consort and not king.)]

who was an American woman, although it sounds much more like a boy or a baseball player.

Emily is an unhappy name and Robinson also, which has

caused her to move from her old room to a smaller one in the rear of the house.

Those poor birds which lived in Mr. Croft's hedge were also forced to move after living there for two to four decades in the hedges which Mr. Croft planted many years ago. The good Reverend says that the society which prevents cruelty to animals could do nothing about it on the whole,

[I was, unfortunately, put in the awkward position of having to tell Mrs. King a little prevarication. When the Robinsons began to remove the hedges in late November, Mrs. King became very much concerned about the sparrows which she quite erroneously believed were nesting there. She suggested that I call the S.P.C.A. to ask for help. However, since the birds were not nesting and since I did not wish to become involved with the Robinsons and since I was positive that the S.P.C.A. could and would do nothing about the hedge removal, I felt justified in telling her nothing could be done.]

and they can look into the entire side of her house which used to lie next to Mr. Croft's hedge.

Constant change is a very bad thing for anyone as old as she is, and it is very upsetting, which does not allow her to think seriously and with composure about her vignettes. We have always objected strenuously to merely listing everyday occurrences, which tell one nothing about the hidden meanings of the things which happen and which relate to the larger purposes of the Lord and the good Reverend, whom she has been unable to see as often as she would like because of sickness and strain discussed in previous vignettes.

[The entry alluded to here was probably one of her best. It is a pity that it was stolen.]

Her son has been unable to see the evil which may be contained in a name, and Alfred is also the name of a great English king and professor,

[Probably Alfred the Great who, although very learned, was not, as Mrs. King suggests, a professor.]

as Edward, her son, informed her and a further namesake of his called Edward the Confessor, whom we do not believe was a Catholic or a criminal. As the good Reverend says, the purpose of confessing is because he despises eavesdropping, as she does and Edward, who merely enjoys being in the dining room and has nothing to do with the name of Emily since it reflects corruption.

Of course, his bedroom is much the same, being on the other side of the house with a wall which cannot be torn down or die.

DECEMBER 15, 1960. [*Mrs. King*].


It was, of course, very kind of the good Reverend to bring us
a tree

> [It had been my custom since the disappearance of
> Lawrence King to purchase a tree at Christmas and
> bring it to the house where the three of us usually
> decorated it together. This was, I believe, one of the
> highlights of Mrs. King's year, so the reader can
> imagine how surprised I was when Edward told me
> that she would be unable to participate in our little
> tree-decorating party. At this time, however, nearly
> two weeks had passed since I had seen Mrs. King.]

and to help Edward, her son, decorate it, because she was not
able to be in the library because of strain. However, when
he comes again she feels it is her duty to see him in order
to discuss the unhappiness and sorrow which she incurred in
Emily, who lives next door, when Mr. Croft was such a good
neighbor, who did not remove his hedges and managed to stay
in the house where Edward could not see him.

The tree is a very important part of Christmas and Christmas festivities, of which we have very little, and no one but the
good Reverend ever comes, because Christ was crucified on
one by the Jewish cavalry without any branches.

> [I grant that this sentence makes very little, if any,
> sense. Mrs. King seems to have confused "cavalry,"
> that part of a military force which usually serves on

horseback, with "Calvary," the hill upon which Christ was crucified. This particular confusion is usually reserved for children of Sunday School age. There also seems to be a second confusion in Mrs. King's mind about the Christmas tree, which, I believe, is a German custom, and the cross, sometimes called a tree, upon which Christ was crucified.]

May the Lord help no one new to come to us this Christmas. Amen.

DECEMBER 18, 1960. [*Edward King*].


A Christmas Play for Children
or
Black and White Sunday

[This is another of Edward's fictitious little dramas in which the reader should place little or no credence.]

(The Christmas curtain opens on the Dining Room, home of Edward Excellent, the Provençal troubador. We see Señor Excellent, guitar in hand, standing beneath Emily's balcony. This can also be read by those of little faith: We see Edward standing at the Dining Room window looking at the Robinson house. Señor Excellent sings.)

> Dingle balls, dingle balls,
> Diddle all the way.
> O, what fun it is to ride
> On one coarse Emil-lay!
>
> Dashing through the snow
> (I am white as snow)
> Making Em-i-lee
> O, what fun we'll have, we two
> You just wait and see.

(Señor Excellent turns to the audience, placing his guitar on the table.)
SEÑOR EXCELLENT: No doubt, you are puzzled because I referred to my True Love as coarse in the course of my song. Of course, I (he gesticulates wildly at himself with both middle

fingers in order to express confusion, excitement, shame, and self-reproach) do not think she's coarse. But others do. (He flings himself on his guitar as if to ravish it and then sits up abruptly with an expression of intense pain on his face, indicating that he has caught his member between the strings.) Divine Retribution! Obscene Castration! She . . . is . . . *not* . . . coarse! And, what is more, it is pure foolishness to attempt to express more than one point of view in a simple love lyric consisting of only two and one-fourth quatrains. (He is about to sing again when he hears the click of the locked Dining Room door. Next the handle is rattled furiously. Then wild pounding.)

A VOICE:

[This "voice" is supposed to be that of Mrs. King.]

Edward, Edward! I heard singing in there. Let me in. Why is this door locked?

[Mrs. King did confide in me later, when Edward was out of the room, that he had locked himself in the dining room. This seemed to bother her very much, since she felt that it indicated he thought his privacy might be invaded.]

Why have you locked me out? Your poor mother? What have I done to deserve this kind of treatment at your hands? (Edward's guitar becomes invisible as his eyes fill with tears. He speaks.) Mother.

A VOICE: Let me in. Let Me In! LET ME IN!

EDWARD: Yes, mother. (He goes to the door and unlocks it. Lady Ears, the mother of Señor Excellent, enters and searches madly about the room.)

LADY EARS: I heard singing . . . and VOICES in here and I heard you say . . . EMILY!

EDWARD: I was only singing Christmas carols.

LADY EARS: Not Carols, Emil-lays.

[Purely fictitious. As long as I knew Mrs. King, a pun
never once crossed her lips. If Edward wanted to
make this dialogue at all realistic, and it is best that
he did not, he should have given himself this particular line.]

EDWARD: No. "Jingle Bells." You must have mistaken "one
horse open sleigh" for "one coarse Emil-lay."

LADY EARS: Coarse? COARSE? Coarse is too mild. Slut!
Wh°re! Hitler! Communist! The good Reverend . . .

EDWARD: You have gone too far. That last term of opprobrium
has decided me to defend my True Love to the very death!

LADY EARS: (Screams and faints on hearing "True Love.") Ar-
gapueyfug!

EDWARD: The pen, or tongue, is mightier than the sword. Lo, I
have matricided with a word or two, one of which rhymes, it's
true. Word or two. Rhymes, it's true. Dum, dum, dum; doo,
doo, doo. (The ballet sequence follows wherein Edward pir-
ouettes around his fallen mother. Finally, after ten hours of ab-
sorbing choreographic pyrotechnics, he rushes over to her and
figuratively throws himself down beside her, indicating with a
complicated series of hand gestures that he is wrong and she is
right.) Ah, faithless me, was not one love enough? (A pause.)
To be or not to be, that . . .

LADY EARS: That is quite enough! (She rises like Venus from
the sea, gracefully, the Earth Mother Eternal.) I would never
have believed it unless I heard it with my own ears.

EDWARD: (Prostrating himself at her feet.) No, mother. It
isn't true. Only you, mother, only you. To me, she, Emilee, is
only the negative of your lovely picture. Her black negative,
your white print. Like a black and white sundae.

MOTHER: White is the color of Sunday and weddings. Monday is blue, Tuesday is violet, Wednesday is orange. Thursday is . . .

EDWARD: Don't say it. Sunday *is* white! How could I have been so miserable as to have forgotten?

MOTHER: And so is Lord Henry.

EDWARD: Yes, so he is, yes, of course, mother. And she is only your negative.

MOTHER: My negative? (She begins to get the idea.) Of course, refined versus coarse, black versus white . . .

EDWARD: Yes, yes, O, yes! Black and White. Night and Day. You are the one. I'm dreaming of a White Christmas. Just like the one I used to know. How could I have been such a fool? I'm not a fool over you.

(She goes to the window and pulls down the shade with gentle vehemence.)

MOTHER: There, Edward, my son. Let that put an end to all this foolishness. And now let's you and I go into the library and sit around the tree.

[This is the Christmas tree which I had decorated for the Kings a few days earlier.]

EDWARD: O, Tannenbaum!

MOTHER: And if you feel like singing, you may sing to me. Something religious, perhaps.

EDWARD: Keep the Christ in Christmas. Keep Edward in the library. Keep the Dining Room window shade pulled. This play just reeks with morals, and I'd like to take this opportunity to recommend it to grammar school dramatic coaches the world over. Edward Excellent is dead, and the son is born!

Only four more days until Christmas, that glorious day which brings joy into the hearts of all. She, of course, does not entertain officially, but the good Reverend, who knows no bounds, is always kind enough to bring a turkey, which he helps her to prepare

> [Of course, I feel that it is the woman's place to be in the kitchen and not the man's. However, preparing a turkey, as I well know, is a very difficult task and one which Mrs. King could not very well handle alone. Since Edward was no help, I sacrificed my principles and annually performed this little service in Christian charity.]

for Edward's sake, because Christmas, in at least one sense, is especially for children, and Edward, her son, loves turkey, which is a bird killed by the Puritans, among which were some of her oldest and most respected ancestors, who later fought in the Revolutionary War, when George Washington spent his Christmas at Valley Forge, which is usually much colder than San Francisco, which has fog.

Christmas time is a time for love and charity, the giving of gifts and presents to those around one whom she loves. She, of course, has only Edward and the good Reverend to whom she gives a check

> [Mrs. King was always very generous in her Christmas gifts, which I always donated to the church, not

knowing what to do with such a sum myself. I never mentioned this to Mrs. King, because she always insisted that I spend the money on myself, and I did not want to hurt her feelings.]

because Edward has no use for money and for whom the good Reverend usually brings something nice, which she has instructed him to buy. This year she told the good Reverend to bring an ivory chess set because the old one

[This set was said to have belonged to Czar Nicholas I of Russia. Unfortunately, either Edward or his mother burned it a few days after Christmas.]

is very nearly worn out, and the black queen was burned in the fireplace in the library.

Edward, too, as good sons should, usually arranges for the good Reverend to bring something for her, and she cannot help but be curious every year as to what this something is going to be. Last year, she believes it was, he gave her a peignoir and a book of verses by Mr. Stevens which she wore but did not understand, since Edward has such a fine mind and reads more than is good for his eyes.

This year Edward has suggested that she serve the good Reverend a drink

[At this time I did not indulge in any alcoholic beverages. Since then, however, I have taken to drinking a glass of Bernkastler Doktor with my meals on the advice of my doctor. It is interesting to note that this same wine was prescribed for Prince Albert, the husband of Queen Victoria.]

to celebrate, but the good Reverend does not drink and does not like the Russians, who cannot grow wheat because they collect it and should starve, so we will have cider instead of Molotov cocktails, as Edward has just said.

The tree, of course, is lovely and the candles, instead of lights, were such a clever idea and an old-fashioned that we cannot thank him enough for bringing back her happy, pampered childhood to her and the many memories which lie put away in her mind.

She remembers the pony

[Apparently a pony which Mrs. King was given in her childhood.]

especially well and wishes that Edward might have had one himself, but the good Reverend says that one may not have one in the city, although she did when she was a girl, which Edward is not, and would be difficult to feed.

In closing, she would like to add that it will be another old-fashioned Christmas with just the three of them again sitting around the house. Because of having to prepare little things, she may not be able to return again for a vignette as is her custom until after the holiday. Merry Christmas, readers, if there are any.

DECEMBER 23, 1960. [*Edward King*].

[Of all Edward's entries, this one is, I am sure, the worst by far. The fact that it is fictitious is proven by its having been written on the 23rd of December when it is not supposed to have taken place until the 24th. I am including it against my better judgment and with the strong recommendation that the reader overlook it. I have only read it once myself in order to ascertain its contents, and I have not seen fit to annotate it beyond this one note, since further annotation would lend it a certain amount of dignity, and this is surely not what it deserves.]

'Tis the night before Christmas and all through the house we are planning our annual Christmas Gala. Tomorrow at 9:00 A.M. or so, Sainted Claws will arrive with the bird:

SAINTED CLAWS: Ah, Mrs. King, I have the bird for you.

EDWARD ELF: No, sire, I have the bird for you. Let me give *you* the bird. (He gives the bird to her, and he gives the bird to him. Those who have received the birds go to the kitchen to prepare them. He who has not received a bird adjourns to the library, not to the dining room, that Forbidden Eden where Adam fell and the shade was pulled on Paradise. Edward Adam lights the candles on the tree arsonistically and sings.)

O Tannenbaum, Irving Tannenbaum
Wie treu ist deine Seder?
Dein Geld ist grün im Sommerzeit,
Und auch ist grün im Winterzeit.

O Tannenbaum, Irv Tannenbaum
You circumcized masturbator!

(Turning to an audience of thousands, Edward Hater explains that it is always necessary to deprecate people of Jewish or little faith during the Christmas season as an extension of Christian charity, which is not to be extended beyond Christians. Next Edward Solomon wisely falls asleep and dreams of the Queen of Sheba, who in a game of somnolent chess, has replaced the cremated black queen. The Black Queen mates the White King, who wets his whistle. Suddenly there is a castanet crescendo. Veloz Perkins and Yolanda King enter the library in the passionate abandon of the Christmas Tango. They dance past Edward the Wise toward the fireplace where the flames of their furious passion blend with the lesser flames of the ordinary, domestic Yule log. A death! A death! A Rebirth! Veloz speaks, addressing Edward the Dispossessed.) You fool, you see I have stolen your mother away from you. All your endeavors have been in vain. Our love is stronger than the Church. And, what's more, we are planning to turn our eyes away from God for a few minutes, so be so good as to turn your eyes away from us, lest they melt in their very sockets.

ST. EDWARD THE FAIR: Sin, you filthy lurch-leaving churcher, may you burn forever in the hot winds of your lust like my friend Dante's friends, Paolo and Francesca.

VELOZ VITRIOLIC: Don't shout foreign swear words at me in Russian. Let it be known, irregardless, that I am a candle and your ex-mother is a lantern.

EDWARD THE VULGAR: Well, it's light up time.

YOLANDA YELLOWING: O, f*cky-ducky-doodle, let it be known that I have been reborn in the arms of this lamb. We are moving away forever to an apartment with or without a view, as the case may be.

EDWARD THE EX: Have you, cold-hearted one, forgot the yearly Christmas midnight pilgrimage to the cellar?

**YOLANDA YELLER:** Cellar, H*ll, cell, you mean, the poisoned prison of our pristine *paterfamilias.*

**VELOZ:** Please, precious, d*mn it, let's not begin life together alliterating ourselves to death.

**YOLANDA:** I have stuffed my conscience into the bowels of a dirty bird for you, and you condemn me for waxing poetic. (She weeps.)

**EDWARD THE PROFESSOR:** Be careful, Ex, lest you wax too poetic and he polish you off. (Edward turns to an audience of millions and explains that he has learned from Shakespeare that an intelligent character always extends the metaphor of the speech which precedes his. He also notes his facile handling of the subjunctive and repeats his speech in case anyone missed it.) Be careful, Ex, lest you wax too poetic and he polish you off.

**VELOZ VICIOUS:** Speaking of Shines, sweets, we now leave you to wallow in the wealth of Ebony Emily.

**EDWARD THE EXEMPLARY:** Do not, foul fiend, destroy my hypothesis by picking up on my metaphor or refer to my True Love in slang terms which express contempt for members of minority groups. Follow my example. Do I not always refer to Huckleberry Finn's friend as Negro James, and did I not change the title of my copy of Conrad's novel to *The Colored Person of the Narcissus?*

**VELOZ VENEREAL:** Speaking of the members of minority groups, is it really true . . .

**YOLANDA YEARN:** Oh, it is! Fantastic difference and so exciting. Why I just, well, good G*d, man, didn't you, too much, to think that, O wonderful!

**VELOZ VIGILANT:** And . . . how . . . would . . . you . . . know?

**YOLANDA YIELDING:** Ah, I was a nurse once, a registered nurse with a pedigree. What I mean is, I used to give enemas for charity. In the slums, you know, lots of them live there, men, boys, *et cetera, et cetera.*

VELOZ VEXED: I believe you. Your millions have convinced me that you could not tell a lie.

YOLANDA: Yes, I could not tell a lie. I am a good buy.

EDWARD: By all means, goodbye to you both, good riddance, and good luck. I, for my part, shall marry Emily Robinson, and we shall support ourselves on our joint annotations to the *Shepherd's Calendar*. Goodbye, goodbye, goodbye. (Here Edward is rudely awakened by his beloved mother, who is attempting to pour a glass of hot, spiced cider down his throat.)

MOTHER: Who were you saying goodbye to, Edward? You must have been dreaming, dear.

EDWARD: Oh, to the old year, mother. It's almost the new.

A.S.P.: Yes, friends, another year has passed, and we find ourselves once again gathered around . . .

EDWARD: An old corpse and sucking the life blood out of it.

MOTHER: Yes, dear.

EDWARD: But I was dreaming. I dreamed about you and our little friend here. You and he were going to this little town somewhere in Kansas to pay your taxes, and you, mother, were with child. And then you weren't with child any more. The child was lying in a manger, and it was me. Some fat old fags in costume were bringing me presents, Frankenstein and Merde, I forget the other one's name.

MOTHER: How nice, a Christmas dream. Do you think it has any significance, Reverend? I mean do you think Edward is the Messiah?

A.S.P.: O, by all means, and I'm Jesus Christ.

EDWARD: One of us is an impostor. Why don't you be John the Baptist? Your head's never been of any particular use.

MOTHER: Children, children, not on Christmas Eve. Let's sing a song.

EDWARD: (Singing.) "There's place in France where the women wear no pants, and they dance glass so the men can see their Perkins."

MOTHER: I meant a Christmas carol.

A.S.P.: (After some thought.) Really, this is too much.

MOTHER: Oh, don't you like to sing?

A.S.P.: No, I mean Edward.

MOTHER: Oh, Edward loves to sing. Don't you, dear? (They sing, joined by a chorus of angels. A bright star shines down on the house. It is a grand Christmas. The End.)

DECEMBER 26, 1960. [*Mrs. King*].


It was, as usual, a happy and joyous Christmas and, as Edward so happily pointed out, not unlike the earlier and first Christmas when Christ was born as an infant and not a general like MacArthur, who would have bombed the Romans with nuclear submarines, which would have been good enough for them, as the good Reverend says. We had our tree, as mentioned before in these vignettes, with its star, not unlike that of Bethlehem, and Edward, being the youngest, was, of course, Jesus. Since we are his mother, we were Mary, and the good Reverend, who is not Edward's or Jesus' father, was Joseph. It is always well to incorporate religion into one's everyday life.

[I did make some such remark during Christmas dinner. Had I known that it would be given this kind of interpretation, I would have thought better of it. Mrs. King is, I am sure, innocent of any blame in the matter. These perverted ideas are Edward's without a doubt.]

Just to go to church on Sunday, even if one does not, is certainly not enough.

There were, of course, no shepherds. This does not need to be explained. The three kings who brought presents were also not here, but Edward suggested that since he and she were kings, patronymically or some such, they would only need a third king to make a total of three. Edward, as well as she and the good Reverend, of course, know that the third king was a Blackamoor, and Edward was clever enough to suggest Mr. or

Dr. Robinson for the missing king. Kindly enough, the good Reverend pointed out that Mr. Robinson could not participate because we never have guests of any color in the house. Also Emily would have wanted to come, and we cannot have that because of the great danger of interracial marriage or intermarriage, and the black king did not bring his daughter for Jesus to marry, or he could not have been the Savior. It is wise of Edward, her son, to keep an eye on Emily from the dining room window so that she will not inadvertently marry him against his will. But we wish he could occupy himself in some other way, for like most women, Emily may be cleverer than some men.

We have tried to love her and them all as neighbors, even if it is unwise, but we cannot love them as a member of the family. Edward does not love her. He is only afraid she will marry him. He, Edward, is old enough now, and she does not have to sign any of the papers, and she would not if she did. Edward must stay so that she can take care of him. The Robinsons will take care of her, and Edward would not even want to kiss her on the lips.

Why do they not send her away to school where she can meet some nice colored boy of her own race, even if they will have too many children because they do not have any outside interests, or is she too young, but she goes and comes with books everyday? Edward told her. And she hopes that she is not stealing them because it would be a great shame and embarrassment for the police to be in this neighborhood, because this can only happen in a true slum.

We have prayed and prayed that the Robinsons will go back to the Fillmore district to be with their own kind because we do not need doctors in this neighborhood, but there where there is so much sickness and diseases of all kinds, and Emily could be a nurse, dedicated and famous like Florence Nightingale, and not worry about a white husband and father for her children, unless young doctor Malone.

The good Reverend has told her not to worry or become upset over such a stupid matter, and she has not, although it is a
mother's duty to worry and become upset over the future of
her son,

[One might ask oneself what kind of a future Edward would have had.]

especially if she is older than he and if he is about to make
a serious mistake which will ruin him and the family. If
only we had taken some soup to Mr. Croft to keep him alive
long enough for the Robinsons to have found another house.
Why, we ask ourselves, do those people in New York want Edward to marry Emily? Are they relatives of hers or of Mr.
Croft's who do not know that she is white? If the good Reverend will give her the address, we will write to them and tell
them.

[Mrs. King asked me for the address in question on
any number of occasions. Each time I attempted to
explain to her that the Kraft executors were in no real
way connected with the Robinsons and that a letter
to the former would be of no use whatever. Each
time she seemed to understand and would drop the
matter until I visited the house again. In her diary I
found the following letter on a loose sheet of paper.
It has no date, address, closure or signature:

"Dear Sir,

"We hasten to inform you that Edward King
is white. He cannot and must not marry your relative,
Emily Robinson, whom you no doubt know is black.
Why you persist in this matter is a mystery. You must
know that no good can come of it and that you are
breaking the heart of an old and aging lady who has
always done her best to love her neighbors as herself.

Anyone can make a mistake, and so we forgive you. Please be so kind as to move the Robinsons to another neighborhood where they will be happier."

I conclude from the straightforward syntax of this letter that Mrs. King spent a good deal of time working on it. One wishes that she had spent a similar amount of time on her diary.]

Then, surely, they will not press the matter, having been informed of the true nature of the case. We pray and pray for guidance from the Lord, thanking him all the time for such happy moments on Christmas, but we grow worried that as Edward approaches the exciting age of thirty-five, he will decide to begin life with someone new. Helen Trent was a woman and had no aging mother to contend with, and they all were white, so things did not make a great deal of difference even if she did not marry him before the tubes blew out. Edward is guiltless, we know. And no blot stains the good Reverend's soul since he is a bachelor. She, too, hopes to be ever more perfect in the sight of the Lord and that the Robinsons will not burn in hell. Amen.

[This is not the first of Mrs. King's entries to conclude with an "Amen," and it is not the last. The reader will see that, as she approached the end of her life, Mrs. King tended to make her entries into prayers. At one time I thought about publishing her diary alone under the title *Letters to the Lord*, but this would have meant that I would have had to publish Edward's diary separately as well. One of my colleagues suggested that I do so under the title *A Soul in the Hands of Satan*, but I gave up this idea, believing that Edward's diary is worthwhile only in so far as it illuminates his mother's.]

Darling Mother,

[In this "epistle" to his mother, Edward attempts to be poetic and only succeeds in being maudlin. I am pleased to think that his mother never read it, but I cannot help but wonder what she would have thought of it if she had.]

It's New Year's Eve and I'm writing a letter to you you'll never read. You are wrong, you know. Emily doesn't love me. She doesn't even know I exist, or, if she does, she only knows a face in the window, a face which probably scares the h*ll out of her. Imagine what it would be like to live next door to us. This big, crumbling old house, the shades pulled, occasional muffled sounds, a single light upstairs late at night, no one coming or going except Perkins with his undertaker's suit and smile.

[A person in my profession must always do his best to keep smiling. It is the shepherd's duty to inspire confidence in his sheep even when the wolf is at the door, as it were. In this way, we are not unlike show business people for, no matter what we feel like inside, the show must go on, if I may borrow a phrase from that other profession. All clergymen must, of course, dress conservatively. Edward surely knew this. I cannot see why he chose to attack my manner of dress, since I always endeavored to appear neat and clean. This is a good deal more than could be said for him.]

I imagine she's just dying to rush right over here and throw her arms around my neck. Even the little kids won't set foot near this cemetery we call home. I'll have another drink on that one, another shot of Old Embalming Fluid, also bottled under the name of Old Massage. It helps to preserve the corpse you think Emily loves.

But, no, mother, the whole thing takes place in my mind. Emily is like a movie star, and I sit in the dining room and watch the show. I fall in love with the heroine on the screen, and when I pull the shade, the movie goes on in my mind. Very simple. Very stupid, I suppose. And so sad it calls for another drink to celebrate the Old Year. The Year of the Robinsons and of Emily. So in this movie, I'm constantly watching it and producing it, I am Solomon and she is Sheba—it's a color film, after all—and very repetitive, very boring, very spectacular. It doesn't have a plot, and it doesn't have an ending. It just goes on and on like this letter won't because I can't even finish it. Even the alcohol won't make it flow because there isn't anything to say, except Emily doesn't love me, mother. She doesn't even know I exist. Can you understand that, mother? Nothing goes out this window to her, nothing but a pale face behind these dirty curtains in half light—a face she probably doesn't even want to see.

JANUARY 1, 1961. [*Mrs. King*].


That naughty boy of hers does not feel altogether too well today.

> [Edward was actually quite ill for the first two weeks in January. I believe he may have had pneumonia, but, for obvious reasons, neither he nor his mother would hear of having a doctor in the house. I recommended the forced fluid and aspirin cure used by our Armed Forces. It seemed to do the trick, as it were.]

He stayed up last night celebrating the New Year and did not tell her it was New Year's Eve, and she, old and aging as she is, completely and wholly forgot. Not like the happy days of childhood and youth when she was always up dancing until dawn without any time to make her New Year's resolutions until days later. Naughty Edward, celebrating all by himself! If only she had known, we could have had a little party for ourselves, and she could have watched Edward to see that he did not become quite so ill and sleep all night on the dining room floor without a blanket where she found him sleeping and shivering this cold morning.

> [I convinced Mrs. King that she should not blame herself for Edward's folly. He was indeed old enough to know his own bedtime.]

She hopes other mothers, who may or may not read these vignettes, will not think that she has neglected her poor, naughty son, who is now upstairs in his own little room asleep with a bad cold which rest and hot tea, which she has made him, will help to cure. But mothers do so love to take care of their little sons.

Perhaps, if she had not moved her bedroom to the back of the house, she would have been awakened by the party which Edward said the Robinsons had, which lasted very late and was very noisy and loud. The good Reverend would not have approved because there were white people there and everyone was doing African dances to African music,

[If the Robinsons wished to have an integrated party, that was, of course, their concern. I have never thought very highly of dancing, and I find the new dances appalling. Whether or not they actually are of African provenance I cannot say.]

not like those lovely waltzes she danced to as a young girl many years before Edward was born.

We are both glad that we did not go to the party, partly because we do not go out and partly because everyone might have become ill and then no one could have taken care of anyone else, and she would have been deprived of the greatest joy of her life, nursing her poor, sick boy back to health.

Edward has asked her not to mention the party to the good Reverend who always spends New Year's Eve in prayer for world peace and the immediate destruction of all God's enemies. But wait, her dear boy calls her.

Sometime later, so to speak. Her dear boy awoke and wanted some more of that delicious tea she prepared him so willingly. He says that he feels better, of course, but she persuaded him to remain in bed for a few days and has carried some of those old magazines in the cellar to burn in his fireplace and keep him very warm so that his cold does not grow any worse.

Perhaps she should spend some of the extra time given her by Edward's illness to compose a few resolutions for the New Year and for the edification of herself and any of the other mothers who might deign to read them if they are ever published.

1. To take good care of her son.
2. To love all the Negroes in the Fillmore district except those who commit crimes and to forgive those when they have been punished.
3. To give the good Reverend extra money so that he will be better able to fight God's enemies, the columnists.

> [Mrs. King no doubt means "Communists," although there are not a few columnists who have helped to destroy a number of traditional American liberties. I do not mention any names.]

4. To read the *Book of Revelations* aloud to Edward while he is still sick as the good Reverend suggested some time ago. When, we cannot say.

5. To pray more and sleep less.

> [The reader must not think that I had anything to do with the latter part of this resolution. Perhaps Mrs. King was still feeling guilty about taking her afternoon nap.]

6. To keep all these resolutions.

Six resolutions are really quite enough for a woman who is aging and who must care for her ailing boy, although he is the first resolution. She might have been wise and prudent to add a seventh resolution not to think about any of the Robinsons and not to worry about their having too many parties and setting the house on fire. The good Reverend says that the Negroes want to set the world on fire,

> [I, of course, only used this phrase metaphorically in regard to the Civil Rights Movement, which seemed, and still seems, to me to be moving much too fast for its own good.]

but surely they would not start with their own house.

Dear Reader, Edward, her son, will probably be waking again soon and will want some more tea, so she must leave this most delightful and fruitful task, admonishing mothers the world over to take good care of their sons on this the first day of the New Year. Amen.

JANUARY 11, 1961. [*Mrs. King*].


Alas, she has been so busy caring for her ailing boy that she
has been unable to sit down and dash off a single vignette
since New Year's Day. A year ago she resolved or made a resolution to write a new vignette every single day except Sunday,
but that became quite impossible, and she is pleased and
happy that she has not resolved to do so again this year. Her
first resolution this year was, as the reader may remember, to
nurse and nourish her son, who grew much worse for a while
but is now getting much better every day and may soon be
up and about again.

The good Reverend suggested that she allow him to bring a
doctor into the house to look at Edward, but we only know
one white doctor, young Dr. Malone, and he does not live in
San Francisco so Edward would not hear of it and said: no, no,
and again, no, bless his heart. He said that he had his own
wonderful and dedicated nurse to take care of his every need,
and he said that he did not even need to see the good Reverend because he was not in any danger of dying and did not
need Extreme Unction from any old priest, the dear boy. He
surely knows that Reverend Perkins is not a Catholic, but he
will have his little joke, which makes him feel better in his ill
health. The good Reverend would not care or mind in the
least.

[Of course, I would not mind if this "little joke" had
been made by Mrs. King. Edward, however, intended
it maliciously and certainly thought I would mind

very much. One can be thankful that Mrs. King was always impervious to her son's malice.]

She has a little secret to confide in the reader of her vignettes, as the case may be. Tomorrow, January 12, 1960, is her birthday, an occasion which her son always tries to make very pleasant for her, sometimes writing a little poem for her like the one she included as a vignette last year, sometimes singing Happy Birthday to her the minute her eyes greet the bright, new day, sometimes making her a little something like the little moth trap in the library,

[This device sat on the mantlepiece. It was made up of a hollow metal tube, a light bulb at one end and an inverted wire cone at the other. The bulb attracted the moth which flew in through a hole at the top of the cone and was thus trapped and soon died from the heat which the bulb generated and the tube retained. On warm summer nights (of which, thank God, there are very few in San Francisco) we would sit in the library with the windows open and no light on but that of the trap, so that Edward could catch moths. His record was thirteen in an evening and he was very proud of it. Even Mrs. King seemed to delight in this vulgar occupation.]

and sometimes having the good Reverend bring her some little, unspecified gift,

[To the best of my knowledge this never happened. Although Mrs. King would always have me bring Edward something for his birthday, he never once asked me to bring anything for her on hers.]

*140*

which she can love and cherish forever. Of course, since he is ill, she cannot expect so very much, but she does know he will remember her with a happy song or verse, if only from his bed. Perhaps we will just play a quick game of Black Swan Hall, which would be very nice.

[Until I read this entry I had never heard either Mrs. King or Edward mention this game. The only information I can give the reader concerning it is that Black Swan Hall is the name of Lord Henry's house in "Our Gal Sunday."]

Because she is a woman, she cannot divulge her age which is a secret,

[Mrs. King was sixty-five on this, her last birthday.]

and she is sure that all will understand this little oddity and eccentricity on her part and forgive her from the fullness of their hearts.

Peace of mind is such a wonderful thing, and the New Year has gone so well, except of course Edward's poor, unfortunate sickness. The good Reverend was so happy to get his surprise,

[I appreciated it very much but thought that Mrs. King could have afforded more than $5.00.]

and the Robinsons, although they are Negroes, have not caused any more trouble so that we have quite forgotten they are even here or there, from the standpoint of the neighborhood, that is. Edward cannot see them from his bed, which is a good thing, and the doors are locked with new bolts,

[Shortly after New Year's Day, Mrs. King asked that I provide bolts for all the outside doors. She would not tell me her reasons, but I suspect that she was afraid of the Robinsons.]

so the good Reverend has to give a secret knock and put a card with his name on it underneath the door before she will let him in.

[I did not bolt the rear cellar door because I was afraid that in case of an emergency I would be unable to get inside the house.]

She must now look into her son Edward's room to see if he needs anything. She hopes it will be all right if she wishes herself a secret Happy Birthday and hopes that the good Reverend does not trouble himself about a gift or flowers or some such.

[Unhappily, I completely forgot the day.]

JANUARY 12, 1961. [*Edward King*].

[In places this entry is so foul and disgusting that I must recommend it be overlooked entirely. I include it only so that I will not be charged by anyone with omitting any part of the diaries which might be prejudicial to me. I pray to God that He will forgive me. I had no choice.]

Everyday in every way I'm getting better and better, but O Emily, my love, I still burn and burn with fever for you, my black rose. For two weeks I have been stashed dying in my room away from you with only my molting nightingale to look at. She's asleep now, my Emily, on her perch, and I've crept down here just to get a fresh look at you—a new vision to content myself with while I play with myself—not that I'd do that in the dining room, Emily, not much. It's too private a single-handed affair for anything but the sick room and, if my Nightingale caught me at it, it might ruffle her feather, and she'd give me away to Pure Perkins, and he'd give a lecture on self-abuse and insanity.

[I most certainly would have, in fact, I would have been sorely tempted to punch him squarely in the face, if such violence can be excused in a man of my calling.]

Is it too cold for you to come out today, my love? I have been waiting so patiently, so like a patient, that is. Shouldn't you be coming home from school soon, or did I miss you already? After nearly two weeks you could at least come out of the house or come to your window, my rose. I need to look at you. Do you ever see me looking? I could play with myself right here, Emily—Onan's tribute to his bride—if Perkins hadn't taken the lock off the door.

[I did this at Mrs. King's request. She was afraid that Edward might lock himself in the dining room all night again and catch a fatal cold. If it prevented him from defiling his own body, praise God. However, merely because he says he did this sort of thing does not mean that he actually did do it. The reader should be well aware by this time that Edward can be and often is a notorious liar. I know no better word for it.]

Strange man, Perkins, he takes locks off one door and puts a bolt on another. The world is now a prisoner outside this house. It can't get in. Even P*ss A*s has to knock now. But he's probably got some door fixed so he can get in if I should be able to convince my nurse not to unbolt for him. He just couldn't stand to be at our mercy.

O, sh*t, I can hear her knocking around upstairs. She'll probably be down like a flash to fetch her delinquent patient when she discovers he's not suffering between the sheets. "For shame, Edward, you know you should still be in bed. You'll catch your death." What do you do with a mother who always wants you in bed? I have sinned in my young life, Emily, but I'd better hide this thing before she catches me at it.

It's almost midnight now, Emily. She's gone to bed in tears for some reason. Is she sad because I'm getting well? Or because she found me in the dining room? She looked at me as if you and I had just announced our engagement, and then she passed out and, revived, passed into the library like a ghost.

This is a madhouse, Emily. It has always been a madhouse, but it used to be a scheduled madhouse. That undertaker you terrified with a smile used to come on fixed days at fixed hours. Now he comes whenever he d*mn well feels like it.

[Because of increased pressure at the church and a number of new community activities, I was not at this time the master of my own schedule. Consequently, my visits to the Kings could no longer be made at their convenience. Of course, I did not neglect them. If anything, I believe that I actually spent more time with them than I had before.]

He even comes in the middle of my mother's naps and wakes her up, and now I won't even be guaranteed two hours of peaceful watching when I am completely well. He must have known I was beginning to enjoy myself. And I will have to let him in, Emily, or he might call the police, pretending he thought something was dreadfully wrong, like we'd been asphyxiated. Wouldn't he love that, though. He thinks he's going to get all our money for his phony church. I'll bet he prays everyday that the house will catch fire and we'll be cremated alive because we're too good, too other-worldly for this world, which reminds me of a little story of another holy man who always made sure that those who were too good always went away to heaven. And you've been so patient, dear Emily, that I'll tell it to you along with my plan for conquering the world and making you my empress.

It seems there was this guy, St. Hilary of Tours or some such place, who thought his wife was too good for this world, and he prayed that she would go to heaven, soon. And lo and behold, she died the very next day. And then it dawned on him that his daughter was also too good for this world and he prayed and it worked again. The Pope, who didn't care much for Hilary, called a council and didn't invite him. But Hilary went anyway, and when the Pope stood up to make a speech, Hilary pointed a finger at him and, lo and behold, the Pope promptly sh*t himself to death. Hilary really had a firm hold on his buddy God's ear.

So what I want is a patent on Hilary's Vatican trick, e.g., you point one finger at a person and, lo and behold, he p*sses his pants. You point two fingers and he sh*ts them. Three fingers and he lets go with the works. You could rule the world with this simple, saintly trick. For example, imagine our late friend, Adolf Hitler, giving one of his rousing speeches in full dress uniform. I am standing quietly in the audience, raising my arm and saying *"Heil"* along with everybody else. Things go on like this for awhile and then I raise my *Heil* hand and give him one finger. His self-confidence is somewhat reduced and he begins to wonder just how he is going to leave the podium. The General Staff wonders why the *Fuehrer* is standing in a puddle of water, and Herr Goering asks Herr Goebbels if Herr Hitler *hat pissen gegangen*. Herr Hitler hears the stir behind and breaks into a cold sweat to match his cold *Hosen*, but he manages to get out one more rousing, *Heil*-producing point, and I give him two fingers. *"Mein Gott in Himmel,"* says Herr Goering, sniffing religiously and examining the fresh stain on Herr Hitler's *Hosen, "Der Fuehrer hat schiessen gegangen."* By this time Herr Hitler has lost a good deal of the General Staff's respect and most of his self-confidence. You can take it from there. Anyway, it isn't long before I'm ruling the world because only me and my captains can hold their own on the platform. But, dear Emily, this is the stuff that dreams are made on, and as things stand I could only use this great gift on the good Reverend, and all it would do for him is change the orifice through which his soul and wisdom flow out. I hope I didn't bore you with my story, Emily, I just wanted you to know that I am not without my dreams, and would you even want to be Empress of an empire built on sh*t?

O, Emily, my rose, you'd think I was insane if you ever read this. But I don't have anything else to tell you. Nothing happens to me that hasn't been happening for the last ten years. I did get sick, though, and I ran a very high fever for a few days. It's the first time I've ever felt warm, and I drank lots of water and had to p*ss into a can because the toilet upstairs is broken, and Perkins, with all his great talents, is no plumber. The lights in your house, in *your* house, have all gone out. Our house is decaying, and it's cold in here, Emily. When will I see you again?

[UNDATED. *Mrs. King*].

[It is my guess that this entry should be dated January 13th. In her diary, it follows after the entry of January 11th and immediately precedes that of January 23rd. Since the volume she wrote in was bound, there is no chance that an entry could be placed out of order.

I have settled on the 13th as the most likely date because I visited the Kings on the evening of that day around 6:00 P.M., after an absence of several days. When I arrived, I learned from Edward that his mother had been locked, barricaded is a better word, in her room all day and refused to come out even to eat. Edward seemed worried and claimed to have no idea what was wrong. For the first time since I began visiting the Kings, I went upstairs, Edward with me. After about an hour of constant pleading, Mrs. King agreed to let me in the room, if I promised to see to it that Edward went downstairs and stayed there. He agreed to go, and she let me in, closing and locking the door behind me. I was quite stunned when, after some additional coaxing, she announced to me that Edward was planning to kill her. When I had heard her story through, I was forced to conclude that it was nothing more than the merest figment of her imagination. She, however, clung to her strange idea and made me promise that I would return early in the morning.

She said she was hungry and asked me to get her

something from the kitchen. I talked the matter over with Edward while I was downstairs. He seemed as puzzled and worried about her behavior as I was. I made him promise to spend the night downstairs and returned to Mrs. King's room with a sandwich where I found her asleep on the bed. I wrote her a note to tell her that I would return about 7:00 A.M. the next morning and mentioned that Edward would spend the night below. Then I pinned it to her dress with a brooch she was wearing and left the room, locking the door behind me and shoving the key under it. (To be sure, I did not place any credence in her story, but I thought she would feel better if she found the door locked.) Since I could not find Edward downstairs, I left the house without saying goodbye.

In the morning Mrs. King seemed much better. She was still in her room, but it was not locked when I knocked. I think she had been crying because her eyes were red and swollen. I was, of course, surprised when she asked me if I thought Edward would run off with one of the Negro girls next door. She seemed greatly relieved when I told her such a thought was pure folly and that Edward had often confided in me that he would rather die than leave her alone. (I hope the Lord will forgive me this little white lie.)

She then asked me to bring her some breakfast and I did. I promised to come again that evening and bring Edward up with me. She thought she might be able to forgive him then (for what I am not quite sure), but she did not want to see him all day. She needed to rest and to think, she said.

That evening, with Edward in her room, she cried a good deal and asked him why he had tortured her (her word, not mine) by pretending to forget her birthday. He apologized profusely, claiming that he really had forgotten. (I cannot say whether he was telling the truth, but it probably is not important.) I then suggested that we have a little, belated birthday party downstairs and Mrs. King, after no little amount of coaxing, finally agreed to it. Edward and I did our best to create a party atmosphere downstairs, and Mrs. King came down to several choruses of the "Happy Birthday" song. We then ate some rather stale cake which I had brought the week before. Everything seemed quite all right when I left.

The reader should not, I feel, take this entry too seriously, since it seems to have been written when Mrs. King was under severe, if imaginary, emotional strain. Its tone is very much like the mood I found her in on the evening of January 13th. I assume she wrote it sometime that day.]

Dear Lord God in Heaven Above, never has any mother anywhere, even in all of radio fame and history, been so hurt and crushed to the very marrow of her aging and tired bones and flesh. We have asked ourselves again and again if we have done wrong to take such good care of her son, who, the very minute her back is turned on him to take a much needed and deserved rest, rushed out of his so-called sickbed down to the dining room where she found him with a silly and, perhaps, guilty look lurking on his very face, sitting there doing nothing on her birthday without a song or a poem or even a Happy Birthday for one who has raised him suckling from a tiny infant with loving care and devotion of all sorts in swaddling clothes.

She fears he was looking for that awful fiendish girl, that Negress

[Unfortunately, if we are to believe Edward's last entry, Mrs. King seems to have been right.]

150

not fit to be an upstairs maid in a brohotel

[?]

whom he watches in secret even on her birthday and she may
not have many more, if any. Then, if not now, he will miss her
tender care and loving caresses. What would Lolly have done
if Stella Dallas died? Who will nurse him back to health and
well-being? We ask ourselves. Not that black girl, we must say,
never, never. She would think he was a fool for marrying her
and let him die and poison him just to get his money and just
to tell her friends she had a white husband to whom she was
not faithful and probably both hated and despised.

We are molesting and bothering ourselves with these
thoughts, these cruelties which torture her even on her birthday which he completely forgot, if he really did and is not just
torturing her to make her die so that he can bring that black
Emily or whatever her name may be into her house when she
is dead and not even remembered by a son whom she loved
and cherished and protected from the cruel blows after he was
orphaned either by fate or death in the cellar. Stella Dallas
said she did not expect gratitude from her child, and Sunday
did not once mention her poor mother starving to death in
Colorado where it snows.

We should have listened and taken heed, but we thought
Edward was different, so loving he was, but we were fooled by
her own folly. Only his mother mattered to him and all mothers should take heed from this, her most tragic misfortune, for
at any time or moment a black devil of any name may possess
a son and turn him and his eyes from all who truly love him.

Even the good Reverend, who has always listened to her in
her most dire needs and afflictions, seems not to see the danger
of that Black Emily sneaking into the house late at night even
by means of a ladder to do unspeakable and filthy things to her
son and murder her in her very bed, but not because he has
not been taught better and a mother cannot love her son too

much, until he betrays her, and she is left weak and helpless to fade away and die with no one caring whether or not she lives or dies.

She asks herself, can he be saved? The good Reverend must and surely will help her for he has often talked about salvation,

[Mrs. King means, I believe, salvation from her present anguish, a task I managed to accomplish. She never expressed any true interest in the salvation of her soul, but I am sure that she now is among the Chosen because of her munificence and kindness.]

but she is too weak and tired to do anything. Was not Christmas a happy time, and he did not even care enough not to go into the dining room again, even knowing that it might kill her, for her heart is weak, if not broken. Perhaps, he wants her dead and wants to kill her. It is his plan because she is not black! Such thoughts molest her aging brain and mind!

He could not want to kill her and bury her? Does not the world end when a son kills his own mother, even if that son is Edward? Will not, we ask and pray, the whole world go up in flames? Oh, God, we pray and beg God to help us in this our most dire hour of heart-rending need! Send her, oh, Lord, the God Reverend

[Mrs. King surely means "good," for I certainly never said anything to her that would indicate that I was anything more than a humble servant of the Lord.]

to help her. She cannot write. She cannot ever write again. She can never write again. The last vignette. Readers, she leaves you. Take heed, oh, take heed of any heartless, murder-ridden

son of yours who would murder his poor mother for the love of
a black. . . .

[The penultimate word in this entry is illegible. Mrs.
King surely would not have written the word that
this word most resembles. Furthermore, this is not
her last entry as she claimed it would be.]

Amen.

JANUARY 14, 1961. [*Edward King*].

[Except for brief allusions to the birthday party, the scenes depicted in this entry never took place.]

G*d Almighty d*mn, this house is mad. We (Perkins and I, and may there never be such another "we" again) had to have a Birthday Party for mother last night. Seems her dutiful son completely forgot that auspicious day and, if Perkins remembered, he didn't bother to show—probably didn't want to lay out five bucks of his own (or is it our own?) for flowers.

[This is certainly not true. On my next visit to the Kings, I brought Mrs. King a dozen carnations, her favorite flower.]

I doubt if the party will make the papers even if it was given in the honor of a wealthy San Francisco matron, Mrs. Josephine King, dowager empress and very nearly the last surviving member of the esteemed King clan. The mice beat us to the cake and, judging from the taste of the tea, p*ssed in the teapot. After the caterer left,

[This is a reference to me. I suppose there is some truth in calling me a caterer, although I think Edward means "purveyor," which was, as I may have mentioned before, but one of the many capacities in which I served the Kings.]

I thought all would be well (you see, the B.P. climaxed a tirade hitherto unparalleled in the annals of infantile behavior, the details of which tirade are too long and involved to go into), but Madame my mother would have it not. After all, I had forgotten her birthday and me, her only son and veritable, true companion in her hours of isolation. How could I? How could you, Edward? After all the years I've watched over you like . . . like, well, like a mother hen?

EDWARD: (O so innocently.) Mayhaps you laid a bad egg?

MOTHER: (In tears.) How can you make jokes at my expense when I'm so old, so aging, so near to my final reward and to my maker?

EDWARD: I know, I'm right here.

MOTHER: You're after her, aren't you? Don't try to disguise your innocence by making lewd and filthy jokes at my expense, old as it may be.

EDWARD: After who, after all?

MOTHER: Her. Emily, that girrrllll next door.

EDWARD: Emily?

MOTHER: Emily. Emily Robinson.

EDWARD: After her? I don't even go outside this g*d d*mned house.

MOTHER: But she comes in, doesn't she?

EDWARD: Through the window.

MOTHER: On a ladder.

EDWARD: On a ladder, yes.

MOTHER: O, G*d, G*d! G*d, G*d, G*d! My G*d! O, my G*d, G*d, G*d!

[Mrs. King would never have taken the Lord's name in vain. I trust the observant reader will be on his guard for such telling clues as these, since they are conclusive proof of the falsehood of Edward's accounts of his doings.]

EDWARD: Your record is stuck.

MOTHER: Stuck? I've been STABBED! All my worst, most hor-

155

rible, ugliest suspicions have been confirmed. I shall die. (Clasps her heart and falls over backwards in her chair.) Ruggafach!!

EDWARD: Ruggafach?

[This word may be an obscenity in some language other than English. A man in my position cannot afford to look too closely into such matters, but I have instructed my publishers, should they decide that this book merits translation, to make certain that an asterisk is used if the book is translated into whatever language this word belongs. As things stand, however, I think it would be foolish to make an obscene word out of this one by substituting an asterisk for the "u" of "rugga-" or the "a" of "fach." The Lord knows there are enough obscene words in English already.]

MOTHER: Help me up. No! Don't ever lay another hand on my aging person again. You're unclean, unwashed, un . . .

EDWARD: Circumcized?

MOTHER: O, you filth, filthy filth. The good Reverend will hear about this. I'll . . . I'll tell him everything, every word, every syllable.

EDWARD: And I'll tell him the rest. I'll tell him all about us.

[I doubt very much if there was anything about the Kings that I did not already know.]

MOTHER: About us?

EDWARD: (Firmly.) About us.

MOTHER: He would never . . . Ah, G*d, Edward, my own son, my own dear boy, I've lost my head. How could I have been so foolish? You've just been teasing me about that vile girl. I've been putting words into your mouth, haven't I? Edward?

EDWARD: Yeah.

MOTHER: She's never even been in our house, has she, Edward?

EDWARD: Naahhh. She doesn't even know how to climb a ladder. Them Negroes are so stupid.

[Edward actually wrote "niggers," a word usually used only by lower class whites, and one which I personally find very distasteful.]

MOTHER: I'm so glad, Edward, so very glad.

EDWARD: Why don't you get up off the floor then?

MOTHER: But I *am* off the floor. Whatever possessed you to say a thing like that?

EDWARD: It will make for interesting dialogue in my diary.

MOTHER: You *are* keeping a diary! I knew it. How wonderful. When can I read it?

EDWARD: You can't, I burned it.

[I need not point out that this is a lie of the first water.]

MOTHER: Burned it? Why, whatever for?

EDWARD: It had filthy words in it. Three-letter filthy words, four-letter filthy words, seven-letter filthy words and love letters to Emily.

MOTHER: WHAT?

EDWARD: I didn't send them. I just wrote them.

MOTHER: You wrote them?

EDWARD: That's what the man said. You're really quick on the trigger there, tiger. I wrote them.

157

MOTHER: (Standing up and racing out the door, screaming.) I knew it. I knew it. I knew it. I . . . (The last "knew it" fades off with Mother up the stairs.)
EDWARD: (To himself.) Up your a*s, Cass.

And so our boy, Edward, is left alone in the library of the family home in San Francisco, that sad, empty room which only moments before witnessed one of that Fair City's gayest parties, attended by many of San Francisco's most brilliant elite. Now he has time to think. He thinks about Emily. But does he? No. He thinks about his mother and remembers a time not long ago after old man Croft died when she locked herself in her room for months, and he, Edward, had to conduct all the business with G*d's Little Wiseacre. Somewhere in the luxuriant depths of his fine mind a tiny "no" begins to bud. It grows, it grows with rapidity, with celerity, and with the incredible speed of light, and it blooms forth from his widely stretched mouth in a shout that literally rocks the chandelier: NO!!

While the crystals are still tinkling downstairs, we find our boy upstairs, kneeling in front of his mother's door, the only one he ever really loved. With a voice not unlike that of the feathers of unhatched birds, he says: "Mother?" There is no answer. "Mother, it's Edward." Silence. "I'm sorry." Nothing but the deafening silence discussed so often by poets and novelists. "I've never written a love letter to Emily." More of the same somewhat intensified. "I hate her. The only thing I want to write her is a poison pen letter, but I couldn't mail it."
MOTHER: You could tie it around a rock and throw it through her window, by G*d.
EDWARD: They'd arrest us.
MOTHER: Who?
EDWARD: The police.
MOTHER: O, I don't forgive you. You've nearly killed me again.

I doubt if I'll ever recover. Do you think that girl could have gone on living if Stella died?

EDWARD: Who, Emily?

MOTHER: No, Lolly.

EDWARD: Lolly, who the h*ll is Lolly?

MOTHER: Stella Dallas's daughter whom she loved very much at one time but whom she could never bear to forgive.

EDWARD: What in G*d's name are you talking about? What have you been reading?

MOTHER: The radio.

EDWARD: The radio? The radio is broken, and anyway you don't read a radio. You listen to it.

MOTHER: I can never, never, never forgive you.

EDWARD: Forgive me for what?

MOTHER: For writing love letters to that . . . that Negress.

EDWARD: But I didn't. I didn't. I did not!

MOTHER: I don't believe you. You're lying. You love her.

EDWARD: I DON'T EVEN KNOW HER!

MOTHER: You're lying!

EDWARD: Can't we please just forget about it?

MOTHER: Never, not unless you can prove to me that you hate her.

EDWARD: But how can I do that?

MOTHER: I'll show you. (She opens the door and beckons him to come into her room.)


And so the curtain drops on another day with your favorite couple, Edward and Josephine King, only to rise again the next afternoon. We find the Kings in the dining room this time. Edward is sitting at the table. His mother is at the window.

MOTHER: I don't see anything yet.

EDWARD: She'll come, don't worry.

MOTHER: Well, she'd better, if you know what's good for you. (There is a fifteen minute period of apprehensive silence.)

MOTHER: Well, where is she?

EDWARD: I said she'll come, be patient.

MOTHER: Well, I can't stand here all afternoon. I'm not as young as I used to be. Well . . .

EDWARD: Do you have to begin every sentence with "well?"

MOTHER: Don't try to distract me, I'm watching.

EDWARD: Well, watch.

MOTHER: I don't see her.

EDWARD: I said . . .

MOTHER: You've given her some pre-arranged signal, a light flashing on and off or . . . Wait! Is that her?

EDWARD: (Going over to the window.) Yeah, that's her.

MOTHER: Well, don't just stand there, open the window. (Reluctantly, he opens the window.) Now, you'd better do it. You promised. (An attractive young girl is seen coming up the walk toward the door of the house next door. The scene is tense and pregnant with doors and windows.) Do it now before it's too late.

EDWARD: (Sticking his head out of the window.) I . . . (A pause.)

MOTHER: Do it, Edward, or else.

EDWARD: I HATE YOU, EMILY ROBINSON! I HATE YOU, I HATE YOU! (The girl, with a look of unfathomable surprise and terror, pauses momentarily and then runs into the house. Medusa's twin brother withdraws his head from the window.)

F*ck. Sh*t. P*ss. C*nt. Wh*re. Starch. D*mn. Sn*tch.

[I have left this incredible string of profanity in its entirety (except, of course, for the necessary asterisks) in the hope that the reader will be able to see what depths it was possible for Edward's mind to descend to. I have not placed an asterisk in the word "starch" because, to the best of my knowledge, this word is not profane or obscene. It may recently have been adopted by the world of slang but, if it has, I doubt that Edward would have known it since he had no intercourse with the outside world, as the reader well knows.]

JANUARY 23, 1961. [*Mrs. King*].


It is probably not anyone's birthday today, even in all of radio fame, but once again happiness has descended upon us like an avenging

[Mrs. King had, perhaps, another word in mind.]

angel, and life goes on tranquilly with us very much like Lorenzo Jones and his Belle,

["Lorenzo Jones and His Wife Belle" was, and may still be for all I know, a radio serial.]

although Edward does not, of course, invent things, and her name is Josephine, not Belle, as was the case with the Joneses.

Happiness has come to her again very much like the coming of Spring, which is just around the corner, although it is still January and not yet Ground Hog Day, when he sees or does not see, as the case may be, his shadow. No shadows, however, shroud her life as she begins to see some of the true glories of old age and infirmities in this, the twilight of her spent youth. May these thoughts of Spring and the equally happy thoughts that life can be beautiful bring as much joy to her dear readers as it does to her, who may live in Colorado where the snow causes a later Spring, and poor Sunday's mother

[Mrs. King has made several allusions to "Our Gal Sunday's" mother but, if my memory serves me correctly, I do not think that any mention was ever made of such a person during the course of that serial. To be sure, I had better things to do with my time than sit with an ear glued to the radio, and I may very well have missed something. We should, perhaps, give Mrs. King the benefit of the doubt in this matter.]

dwells in a deep and dismal abyss and chasm of impending winter and doom, waiting for her daughter to arise through the snow like a Spring crocus on a purple visit.

Never fear, Madame, your daughter must in the end, as all daughters must in the end, visit you, and you, too, will reap some of the benefits and harvests of your child in your old age, which is corrupted by the cruel infirmities of years and dastardly winters. Be glad, then, that she has returned to you even after running off to marry a wealthy and entitled Englishman. Others may have been more fortunate than you, others whose children never left the nest to fly off and marry, but Sunday will return and help you shovel away some of the snow that has burdened your heart and clogged your mind for so long. Every cloud has a silver lining, even in the fog!

Dear Readers All, if you are readers, you must know already, if you have not suspected for some time, that her vignettes have not always contributed all the joy which she always intends that they should. Forgive her, and know that sometimes, too, she is troubled and vexed by the trials and tribulations of life, remembering always that Ma Perkins, the sainted mother of the good Reverend who was never mentioned,

[Once again Mrs. King seems to be confusing fact and fiction. If by "mentioned" she means that my name never came up in this serial, the reader will not, I have little doubt, be greatly surprised. Perkins is a relatively common name, especially in the Middle

West and, for what it is worth, I have been an orphan since birth.]

also was not always perfect, although very nearly so because she had to work like a dog in that lumber yard, and her son is better to her than Shuffle ever was, and may the Oxydol sparkle

[The brand name of the washing product which sponsored "Ma Perkins."]

descend into every life to brighten everyone from here to there, and send for the seeds before it is too late, for flowers, even carnations, will brighten every life.

Despair and sadness, the vultures of peace and freedom, may raise its ugly head in any life no matter how wonderful and Christian it is led. As Edward, her own, dear boy, says: Kill it before it eats into your very vitals and wrecks whatever happiness the good Lord has doomed to consider your share, even if you are undeserving.

Happiness is sometimes but a ticket to Heaven, as the good Reverend says,

[I may have told Mrs. King at one time that true happiness could come from knowing that one was assured of a ticket to Heaven. She seems to have twisted my meaning somewhat.]

and it pays for itself in the long run with even greater dividends than some stock we own, if you will forgive such an intrusion of matters of the world into matters of the spirit. These worlds are far apart and, if you remember that, you will be happy, a rare commodity that should be treasured. May God bless everyone on this bright Spring day, even if the sun is not shining. Amen.

JANUARY 23, 1961. [*Edward King*].


Whatever must that poor girl have thought.

[I believe that Edward is referring to his having
yelled out the window at the girl next door. Of
course, this was only a fiction of his own creation. I
find it most strange that he almost seems to have
come to believe it himself. I understand that this kind
of behavior is typical of certain types of insanity, and
the reader will agree, I think, that elsewhere Edward
has shown signs of being demented. It would be interesting to explore this further, but there is little
merit in psychoanalizing the dead, as it were. As it
is, I hope that his soul, wherever it may be, is now
finally at rest.]

It must have been like having all seven vials

[If I did not know that Edward both scorned and, on
occasion, even went so far as to abuse the Bible, I
would be tempted to think that this allusion was to
*The Book of Revelations,* Chapter 16. As it is, I am at
a complete loss to explain what he means.]


poured on at once in some kind of grand atonement for all the
little sins she thinks she's committed. One of these days, when
St. Alfred isn't here to protect us, they're going to come and
collect us and cart us off to Napa

[Napa is the popular name for the state mental hospital located at Napa, California, some fifty miles north of San Francisco. The Kings, it will be remembered, were in a position to afford private care if it had ever come to that.]

to be with our own kind. But now at least I have some peace—

[Can Edward mean that his having thought he did what he did not do actually gave him peace of mind? I should certainly hope not.]

peace at the expense of sanity is our motto here, peace at the expense of sanity, yours and your neighbors'.

I still wouldn't be surprised if the Robinsons packed up and left. Wouldn't that please one and all, though? If Croft hadn't died, things, I say, things might have gone on in the same old way for ten, twenty years. I could have gone through all the books in the attic,

[The reader will remember that Mrs. King mentioned that she had found Edward in the attic reading his father's old books. How much time he spent there I cannot say.]

awarded myself a B.A., M.A. and a Ph.D. and gone off to Harvard

[A well-known college on the East coast.]

to teach Lunatics (that's the subject, not the students). "It gives me great pleasure to introduce to you Dr. Edward King, who for the last twenty-five years has not spoken to a living soul."

[Edward has forgotten his mother and me.]

Or better yet, to some monastary school high in the Transylvanian Alps:

[I have not been able to locate this mountain range on any of my various maps. Perhaps this name is a figment of Edward's always active imagination.]

"It gifes me great bleasure to bresent vrom you Herr Doktor Brofessor Edvart Kink, vhich hass vor de last tventy-fife year been buriet alife in Zan Vranzizco. He iss an an exshpert von blutzuckink unt inzest." And so we see at last that water does seek its own level, that the soul will always return to its native habitat and that Central Europe is the true home of all Western types of insanity. Come to think of it, has anyone ever heard of a Crazy Chinaman? I qualify, therefore: the home of all types of insanity, since the East, mysterious and dark as it may be, seems incapable of going insane.

[Edward seems to have forgotten the behavior of the Japanese during World War II as well as the recent Communist Chinese Revolution and the Korean War.]

O, Edward, my boy, you are a gen-ee-*ss. I had no idea that you were such a deep thinker, such a *Philosoph*. Perhaps God has already granted you a Spiritual Doctorate after only ten years of study. But a doctorate in what, Self-Absorption? Yes, that's it, at last, my salvation: a career in Southern California: Edward King's Temple of Self-Absorption and Peanut Vending. May I send you one of our brochures? "After ten years of isolated self-seeking, I have at last discovered the mystery which formulates the very basis of life, the pivotal point of the body and the soul, the hinge of Good and Evil, the clasp of the Satanic brooch which God wears over his heart. You may well ask what it is, and I tell you it is nothing more than the simple peanut. Eating them, my friends, will help, but by selling them the pivots, trivets, fulcrums, hinges, and clasps of life will begin to be realized for you in your own personal brain. Our introductory course is only Twenty-Five Little American Dollars, and we absolutely guarantee that after vending as little as 100,000 of our peanuts you will realize at least a pivot, trivet, fulcrum, hinge, or clasp or your money back. After that, who knows, the world is yours."

[Where Edward acquired such nonsense is beyond my knowledge and my comprehension. The reader will, I hope, take this sort of thing at its face value.]

But, Emily, what has happened to you? I had intended to write an apology for my insanity, not to prove it to you. But you see, Emily, this diary is my only entertainment, the only thing I can talk to and the only thing that talks back to me later in a language I can understand. Most of the time I'm a ventriloquist's dummy. I sit on my mother's lap and talk to her or yell out the window at you with her voice, or I sit on Perkins' lap

[Edward means this only figuratively. He never once sat on my lap, nor would I have countenanced such an idea if he had tried. What he means by the rest of this nonsense is anybody's guess.]

and talk against him. I mean I can't say anything of my own to him, or he looks at me as if my last marble just rolled out my ear, so I spend most of my time annotating his conversation, if you can call it that. I prefer oration or monologue myself. My mother's conversation isn't even as spontaneous as his, and if you hadn't come along, it would have remained pure, garbled soap opera script. My mother is kind of the lump sum of the dregs of Ma Perkins, Our Gal Sunday, Stella Dallas, Mary Noble, Helen Trent to my Shuffle, Lord Henry, Lolly, Larry Noble, and Gil Stratton. It's her way of creating and organizing a world which started rotting at its very foundations ten years ago. If you knew what I know, maybe you could understand why I did what I did.

FEBRUARY 2, 1961. [*Edward King*].


Dear Emily,

You see this diary business is really turning into "Letters to
Emily." I hope you wouldn't be displeased if you knew.
(That's an odd construction, "I hope you wouldn't be . . ." O,
well.) I owe you something after that scare I must have given
you.

[Edward is still dwelling on his little myth.]

It almost makes me feel guilty. I mean what you got out of it
and what I got out of it. I reread my last entry and feel I
should apologize for being so maudlin. I've got this great ca-
pacity for feeling sorry for myself and

Good G°d, there's a mailman at our door yelling "Special
Delivery."


Is this your letter, Emily? It's got *our* address on the envelope, but "Miss Amelia Robinson." What now, Emily, or is it
Amelia? A midnight trip to your mailbox? It's from New York.
Looks like a masculine hand. A boy friend, brother, uncle,
cousin? Ah, Emily, think what I could learn about you if I
opened it. I can't very well leave the house to deliver it. What
if I got caught on your front porch? I imagine your father
would like to beat the holy h°ll out of me, and I bet you'd approve, too. Not that I don't deserve it. And what if my mother
caught me sneaking back from your house? She'd never believe
it. So what about your letter, Emily? (I like Emily better than

170

Amelia, if you don't mind. Emily is like Dickinson, my soul-sister, and Amelia sounds like some gaudy sea animal-flower type thing.) So, Emily, what about your letter? It has XOOOXXOOXO

> [A juvenile code signifying love and kisses: O = love, X = kiss.]

on the back and no return. I guess that settles the question of who the sender might be, but isn't XOOOXXOOXO a bit juvenile for a boy friend your age? But then how old are you, anyway? Eighteen, nineteen? The letter might mention something about that. The letter, Emily, the letter. I'm going to open it! May God forgive me, it's either that or burn it. I can't deliver it, and I can't burn it.

> [If Mrs. King did not refer to this same letter in a later entry, I would think that Edward was making the whole thing up, creating another phantasy, as it were. If Edward did willfully open a misdelivered letter, he surely must have been aware that he was committing a criminal act which, I believe, is a federal offense. His action is also reprehensible from a moral standpoint. It is possible, however, that Edward actually wrote the letter himself and left it lying around to torture his mother. In either case, he is to be heartily condemned by all right-thinking persons.]

I was right, it is a boy friend, or should I say fiance? Would you like to hear it? *I* will write it to you this time.

"Darling Amy,
"New York is colder than you-know-what. I still haven't found a place to live, so the hotel address still holds. Rents are

incredable [sic] here, and I've got [to] find something soon before school starts. This doesn't give me much time. I'd like to get an apartment so we won't have to look for another place this summer, but the cheapest place I could find was $200 and Dad says that's too much. If your Dad could kick in something later I don't think $200 would be to[o] much, but we can't ask him to do that now. Maybe a room will have to do till June.

"My courses are all set up. English (ugh!), German (ugh?), Chemistry, a sophmore psych course, and some history thing that sounds appalling.

"Anyway, if we are well on our way to being Mr. and Mrs. Roger C. McIntyre, we're a long way from being Dr. and Mrs. Roger C. (They both sound weird.) I've been to Harlem for a quick look-see. Is that place ever a zoo, but the Puerto Ricans seem to have it worse than the Negroes. I even think there may be less prejudice [sic!] against us.

"I've got to be real careful how I dress. If I'm too neat, I look like a Muslim and too messy, well, you know. I met this cat, if you'll excuse the expression, from Africa who has an English accent. He's had most of his schooling in England and comes complete with Oxford accent and the rumpled British look, if you know what I mean. He says he has it much better here than the American 'cousin.' If he has any trouble with a landlord, etc., he just says he's not a Negro (really!) but an African, and unless the guy wants to hear from the embassy, well. So I've been cultivating a French accent for the same purpose, mon chere [sic].

"Well, I should get some sleep and prepare myself for the pavements again tomorrow. Got any ideas for a graduation present for yourself? Clothes are much cheaper here, but cigarettes are unbelievable. Listen to your Dad on cigarettes! Remember that I love you and that I'm counting the days one by one until June!

> "Love and kisses (see the envelope for verification), [signed] *Roger*"

Well (if I may borrow a phrase from our pal, Roger), it seems you've got yourself a pretty nice boy, Emily old girl. Bit of a snob, though, isn't he? About Harlem, I mean. A rose by any other name would still smell like Roger, but that's unkind. I suppose there's nothing in this letter that you don't know already or really need to know, if you don't. Old Rog is still in the same place, and you'll have plenty of time to think about a graduation gift. That makes you about seventeen or eighteen, doesn't it? A little too young for marriage but, what the h*ll, if your folks have money. I bet you're going to be a nurse or a teacher. School for you, too, in New York, I'll bet. Sounds like our boy is a real go-getter, too, no laying in the shade with a piece of watermelon for Old Rog. And I've never even been to New York, Emily, not once.

[This is true.]

FEBRUARY 4, 1961. [*Mrs. King*].


[When I arrived at the Kings' on this day, I found Mrs. King upstairs in a state of near emotional collapse. For three hours I made futile attempts to console her, but she remained completely unresponsive to my efforts. It seems that she had found the misdelivered letter which Edward opened and copied into his diary on February 2nd, and she believed that he had written it himself. Indeed, I did not know until I read his diary that he had not, nor did he at that time make any effort to tell me what had happened. Instead, he met all my inquiries with obscene suggestions and gestures. From Mrs. King, I got little more. She did tell me that she had found a letter Edward had written and, when I asked to see it, she said she had burned it like "they will burn in h*ll." She would not, however, say who "they" were. I then suggested that she confront Edward, but at the mere mention of the name she became hysterical and muttered something about Roger, New York, Amy, and h*ll. When I tried laughing at her, she threw a paperweight at me, so I went downstairs where Edward told me to leave and never come back or he would kill me just as I had tried to kill his mother. When I laughed at him, he threw a bookend at me, so I left the house. Because I was terribly worried that something might happen, I hid in the backyard under a window for a few hours until someone, no doubt Edward, emptied a pot of urine on my head from above. All in all it was a thoroughly disgusting experience, and I was never closer to abandoning my mission. If I had not been so worried about the Kings, I surely would have.]

Life does not begin at sixty-five, although it may or may not begin at thirty-five, but terrible and horrifying things can happen in twenty years

[Mrs. King undoubtedly means thirty years.]

or in one day, which will cause the destruction and damnation of a soul, which for its own sake may burn in h*ll fires forever for lying to his poor and aging, dying Mother. She has found one of his letters to that girl, which he said he did not, could not, and would never write. May he write her then forever from the post office in h*ll where they will live happily ever after.

She is not so stupid and ignorant to be fooled by any amount of disguises or lies, when they wish to run off to New York or some such place together because he says he will never leave the house in a horde of lies for which Judge Pendleton would send him to his very death and burning d*mnation where it is hot, even if New York is cold. And he is Roger, not Edward King, her son, but McIntyre now who is cursed and d*mned for lying and disguising his lies as if no one ever lied to poor Ma Perkins when Sunday ran off with Lord Henry to let her mother die alone in Colorado.

Oh, no, alas, this cannot happen after years of teaching that cleanliness is next to honesty,

[I would suggest that "Godliness" be substituted for "honesty" if it were not reasonably clear that Mrs. King, in some vague way, is discussing truth.]

the chief of the seven deadly

[Surely, Mrs. King means "cardinal."]

virtues, as he once said to her in what may have been a lying tone of voice, while one Amy or Emily or some such black name was laughing up her skirts under the dining room table, waiting for her to leave or die so they might live in peace and prosperity.

Helen Trent never married that no good drunkard and, if she had, her mother would have disowned her, if she had one, or stopped her, if she did not. She has not spent years writing vignettes merely to have him run off with some colored black-guardess, nor has she ever believed that he would not or that mothers of any kind should sit back and allow this kind of escape, once the gory and wretched doom of the lying and disguised plot have ravished the very foundations of her spent youth and been discovered for what those two really are and, what is more, hope to be in New York alone together without her.

She hears the clarinet call

[I would suggest an emendation to "clarion call."]

to action and will not stop now if wild horses drag her through the pinnacles and spines of some great cesspool of quicksand into which they secretly want her to sail, for not once did he mention his Mother to that Jezebel Amy or Emily of a rotting family in the Croft house, and may he burn with them in sulfur and brimstone flames because he drank the soup the good Reverend brought him

[Once again, I must stress that I did not at any time take any soup or anything else, for that matter, to Mr. Kraft, Croft, what have you.]

176

who now refuses to help her and says that her imagination is old and dying,

[What I said to Mrs. King was that I thought her imagination was a bit overworked and that she should be careful not to become so overwrought at her age.]

perhaps to find some place for herself in Heaven, where she belongs after years of caring for him and suffering by herself, misunderstood but hearing the call to action for this treacherous crime shall be stopped.

May the others who read this know it and follow her example, setting fire to the wool pulled over her eyes by them. Goodbye, goodbye, forever, to the world of vignettes and hello, by G*d and h*ll's hot d*mnation, to the world of action forever!

[Although this is not Mrs. King's last entry, she did not pick up her diary again until March 15th. I think it was at about this time that she stopped speaking to Edward altogether and, to the best of my knowledge, she never spoke to him again; at least, she never did so in my presence, and I spent more time with the Kings in February and March than I ever had before.]

FEBRUARY 6, 1961. [*Edward King*].


[By and large, Edward does not vary much from the
truth in this particular entry.]

J*sus G*d, I never thought I'd be glad to see that bastard
again.

[This is the only sign of gratitude I ever remember
receiving from Edward.]

But let me begin at the beginning, if there is one, and end at
the end, if there will ever be an end. Two days ago my mother
found that stupid, g*d d*mned letter that that moron delivered
here by mistake and that I didn't have the common sense, if
sense is ever common here, to burn. I was in the library reading when I heard this glass-breaking yell followed by a dead-
ening thud. I found her sprawled out on the floor of the dining
room with pal Roger's letter tight in her hand. When I revived
her, she started to scream again and screamed for ten minutes.
Then she ran upstairs to her room and locked and blocked her
door, screaming, crying, and muttering all the time. In a
couple of hours, she quieted down, and then Perkins came. She
let him in and started to scream again and screamed until he
left about three hours later. All was quiet again until about
6:00 o'clock last night. I was napping in the library when suddenly there was a great crash of glass in the dining room, followed by another crash a little further away. I ran into the
room and found her with a broom in one hand, and her other
arm was raised over her head. Her back was toward me, and

she was looking out the window she had apparently just broken with the broom handle—why I don't know. The window still worked and even had both its weights. I was about to ask her what in G*d's name had she done, when she pivoted around on her heel like a general and gave me the following speech, which was actually written down on a piece of paper she pulled out of her apron pocket. Since she left it behind in the dining room and I have nothing better to do, I'll copy it:

"You rotten son, Edward or Roger, who cares not for his mother, you had to be stopped by action, not by vignettes or any other such nonsense and morality. We [I gather this is the editorial or regal "we."],

[Edward had apparently never read any of his mother's diaries, otherwise he would have expressed no surprise at her eccentric use of pronouns.]

too, can write letters and we have let them be a letter of truth and honest virtue, next to cleanliness. Your treacherous plot and crime have now been foiled by truth and exposed so that you will burn forever. Do not speak to her again for she has no more words so rotten for you. Thank you. Amen."

(I thought when she read it that "she" must refer to Emily, but apparently it is some sort of female Caesarian third person.)

[The reader, of course, already knows this.]

When she'd finished reading, she went back upstairs and left me to face the consequences of her "action." I ran to the window and saw a large hole in the Robinsons' window opposite. My pious exclamation over this tragedy, and I can assure you it was one, was greeted with pounding at the front door. My heart tried to hump my liver, and I offered a brief prayer that by some vague stroke of luck it might be Perkins, but I opened the door fully expecting to see Mr. Robinson, equipped with a switch-blade and the will to use it. Saints be praised, it was Perkins! I grabbed him by his plastic collar

> [This he actually did, which worried me no little amount at the time, since on my last visit, if the reader will remember, he threatened to murder me if I ever returned.]

and hauled him into the house, giving him a speedy run-down of the situation and ordering him to go next door immediately and rectify whatever had been done. Oddly enough, he went and returned almost immediately to say that no one appeared to be at home. I fainted for a while, just to show my gratitude, and then we kept a silent vigil at the dining room ex-window, scene of past pleasures and present terrors, until ten.

Thereabouts, a light went on in the Robinson house, and my white knight in shining serge went over to "explain." (Whatever that entailed I didn't ask and don't know.)

> [Facing Dr. Robinson was not very much to my taste, since I know what those people are capable of when they have been drinking or are angry. Much to my surprise, he seemed to be very pleasant and accepted my explanation without question. I merely told him that the two lunatics who inhabited the house next door were in my care and that one of them had accidently thrown something through one of his windows. He went into another room and returned with a jar which he gave to me. I offered to pay for the broken window, but he said that he had been thinking about replacing it anyway because the glass was wavy, and it made him sick to look out of it. He then asked if I had thought about institutionalizing

my charges. I said that I had, gave him my telephone number in case there was further trouble, and left.]

He came back about twenty minutes later with a cold cream jar in his hand. The jar contained a note, slightly greasy, which read as follows:

"To Whom It May Concern:
The only place to which they can go together is h*ll. Be it known from one who acts and has never written a vignette in her life, although an unfooled mother.
[signed] J. K."

Together we boarded up the broken window and Perkins left, mother none the wiser. I sat down and cried. How can I go to h*ll, I said to myself: I am there, I am there and only Perkins could know it, if such small facts ever penetrate his skull and smile.

[I was not, needless to say, living in Paradise myself.]

FEBRUARY 16, 1961. [*Edward King*].


Ten days now my mother has been dead and an angel in a heaven of her own creation. She has slain the devil with a rock and has no more intercourse with sin-stained humanity, of which class I am the sole, surviving member available to her. But she does not even see me as she parades through the house in perpetual, if yellowing, white,

[It should, perhaps, have been mentioned before that during these ten years Mrs. King wore nothing but black. I do not know whether this was a matter of taste or if she was in mourning for her husband. However, she changed to white sometime after the unfortunate incident of the window. She did not give any reason for the change, and I thought it would be rude to ask her about it.]

setting her heaven in order with a dust rag.

[For all practical purposes the house had not really been cleaned for ten years. Edward occasionally swept, but to the best of my knowledge, Mrs. King, unaccustomed as she was to menial labor, never lifted a finger in this direction, not that the house did not need it, of course. A cleaning woman would have been out of the question, although I did not once enter the house without the idea occurring to me.]

She speaks only to St. Peter Perkins.

[On my first visit to the Kings after the window incident, Edward directed me to his mother who was in the library. As soon as I was in the room, she locked the door and informed me that there was no one else in the house to speak to. I concluded that this meant she was not speaking to Edward. Not wishing to upset her, I let the matter drop, thinking that things would set themselves right in time. As I mentioned before, I do not believe she ever spoke to him again.]

To him alone do her angelic lips open and then never in my presence. Since he spends all of his time with her, I don't even get to talk to him much beyond "Where is your mother, Edward?" and "Goodbye, Edward. Don't pester your mother while I'm gone. She's still not herself." Not herself? She's dead! I always knew I would miss her when she died, and I do, I still fix her meals, though. I feed the dead, am I not admirable? I used to leave food for Santa Claus and the Easter Bunny, and they'd eat after I had gone to bed, but they'd leave me something in return besides empty dishes and silence.

And Perkins, I never thought I would miss him, and I can't stop him and say, "Please talk to me, I miss you."

[Edward had never shown any great pleasure in my visits, and I was always under the impression that he did not like me very much. Since at this time I had no reason to think he might have changed, I did not spend any more time with him than was absolutely necessary. I regret this now very much. The shepherd should always have an eye for the wayward lamb who wishes to return to the flock.]

I can't yet, anyway, and the earth will crack wide open if I do. It will, I know it will, because that sentence does not belong to me and, if I use it, the world will fall apart, and the sea will burn or, if it comes to belong to me. . . .

G*d knows I never intended to set the world on fire, but I didn't think things would end like this, that I, a mortal, would end up ministering to an angel and to a saint. It's like being caught with your genitals in your hand when G*d pays an unexpected visit, but that doesn't *mean* anything here, nothing *means* anything here. I am dead, too, yes, but I went to h*ll and they went to heaven. I see them, they don't see me. Nobody sees me. I disappeared when we boarded up the dining room window. I sealed myself up inside myself.

I should be able to talk to myself. I went to a good school. I had ten years of internship, but there isn't anything to say, to talk to myself about because I'm not and they're not, either. I shoved everything out of the window and then boarded it up with everything still outside. I have paid dearly for that breath of air which came through the window. I know it's poetic justice. I committed suicide and didn't even know it and now I'm dead, too. I am a tree in the garden of suicides and nobody talks to trees. I am not even as beautiful as a poem. I used to hate that son of a b*tch and now it's all the same, all equal. I can say Dante

[The Italian poet who wrote the *Divine Comedy*, a political satire.]

and Kilmer

[Joyce Kilmer, another poet and the author of "Trees." This poem proves again that there are no atheists in fox holes.]

in the same breath and nothing inside me screams. Can I even say, "Reverend Perkins, sir, please stop and speak to me?" Not yet, but maybe tomorrow. Yesterday, I screamed "Mother,

Mother," and it went through her like nothing, like water through a dirty, white sieve. I suppose I don't even care. My mother in white isn't my mother, and I'm not my mother in a black dress.

[This particular sentence is highly reminiscent of Mrs. King's style. It almost seems to mean that Edward was actually wearing his mother's dresses. Mrs. King once told me that he had done this to entertain himself when he was a child, but one would think that such a practice would have ended long ago. In any event, the sentence is true. Edward was certainly not his mother.]

After all these years and then this.

MARCH 15, 1961. [*Mrs. King*].


This is not a vignette and anyone who says it is is a liar. Too many years listening to the radio and other such fools have nearly killed her, always depriving her of an action. This, then, is an action, even if the good Reverend persists in destroying all her dresses

[A word of explanation is required here. Early in March, Mrs. King presented me with five old white dresses which she wanted me to have cleaned. The gentleman at the first cleaners I took them to refused to take them. He said that they would fall apart because they were so old. When I informed Mrs. King of this, she indicated that I was not telling the truth and insisted that I have them cleaned. Another cleaner accepted them, but only after I signed something which showed that I assumed full responsibility for any damage done. He would not take them otherwise. Only one of the dresses survived the cleaning, and I unfortunately dropped that one in front of a bus as I was returning it to Mrs. King. (I shall not discuss the manner in which she greeted this information.) Fortunately, she had a number of white dresses left, and she insisted on cleaning them herself. Happy to be relieved of this responsibility, I delivered a five gallon can of cleaning solvent to her the next day, and that was the last I ever heard of white dresses, although she continued to wear them.]

in order to keep her from doing her action as she continually plans. It cannot be stopped and will not be, even if several other fools force her to write another vignette. People who live in glass houses should not throw stones, so they had all better tend to their own little businesses and let her tend to hers.

She is sick of vignettes and black dresses. Nothing has been done for so many years because they have kept her a prisoner in her own house, forcing her to write vignettes and do nothing. The action will either be a convent or a coffin,

[I must say that I never really understood what Mrs. King meant by an "action." In the last weeks of her life, this word frequently came up in our conversations, but after an initial attempt to find out what she meant by it, I dropped the subject. She did, however, seem intent upon going to a convent, of all places, and asked me to bring her as much information as I could locate on that subject. I did bring her a few books, but she was not satisfied with them. I tried to discourage the idea, since I did not think that she would be at all happy in a convent. (There was also the problem of what to do with Edward if she went.) She met my discouragements with rage and claimed I was trying to send her to her coffin. When I tried to explain to her that there were a number of other alternatives, she informed me that she was a good deal older than I and knew a good deal more about the world. It would have been unkind of me to argue with her.]

for she is not afraid of either now that she has deserted them, and they have deserted her, hoping to publish her vignettes and poison everyone.

She does not believe the vignettes anymore, since they are all lies and falsehoods which she was forced to write under lock and key because no one would speak to her if she did not. Never, ever again, forever, says she. Let the world write itself vignettes if it wants them that badly. She is going to a convent and then to a coffin along with millions of other tortured women, preyed upon like vultures by various and sundry men, none of which would write a vignette but devoted themselves to the foolishnesses of love letters, trying to capture some poor woman and make her a slave to her pen.

Nothing can stop her now, even if it tried. Never take naps in the afternoon, either, and that is not a moral, it is an action. Never love anyone who makes her write vignettes or listen to the radio if it is broken. Nothing comes of this, and nothing is the greatest and most important answer, if the action is the question she has been asking herself all these years and receiving, mind you, no answer at all. Even Mr. Croft died.

Peace and courage may come in strange ways, and to open the door to them is an action, even if it is only the good Reverend come to take her dresses away and burn them under her very nose and the dangerous wheels of a bus. This is an action and if any fool thinks she does not know, she does, so there.

Remember well that if Sunday's mother had not stayed in Colorado, she would not have frozen to death. Life may be a train ticket to California, if happiness is a bus ticket to Heaven, and she stresses that for all the doubting Thomases who think life is little more or less than a few vignettes, a dust rag, and a lie. They can all, all of them, go to h*ll, and she means it, so there.

There is no hope in this and she knows it, too. She knows it, always letting a smile be her umbrella when it rains the death of sins. Happiness, happiness, happiness, she cries unto herself in the sanctum of the vestibule of her white heart. Let it be known!

[Except for those few annotations I have made, I do not understand very much of this entry beyond the general tone of anger which pervades it. By and large, however, it is fairly accurate in its representation of Mrs. King's conversational attitude in March. I usually understood little of what she was saying to me, and, if I asked her to clarify, she flew into a rage, claiming that I, too, was against her, whatever that might mean. It is possible that Edward was annoying her during my absences from the house, of course, but she never said so specifically or, for that matter, mentioned his name in my presence. It is interesting to note that sometime in March she began to speak of herself in the third person singular as well as in the first person plural. Since at the time I knew nothing of her writing habits, this confused me at first, but I quickly grew accustomed to it after a few visits, just as I had grown accustomed to any number of things which I had never even dreamed would happen to me.]

MARCH 16, 1961. [*Edward King*].


[This is Edward's last entry. I have no idea why he did not write anything for nearly a month or why he stopped writing altogether nearly two weeks before the terrible fire which consumed him and his mother, unless it was because he realized that a blank page, at least for him, was all too often an open invitation to sin.

As the reader will see, Edward seems to be contrite in this, his last entry, if nowhere else. In light of this, I hope that the Ultimate Judgment of his soul was not so severe as one might suspect it would be from reading his previous entries.

At least once a day, I remember both of the Kings in my prayers and give thanks that I, in some small way, have been able to help my fellow man. This is especially important to me now that the state of my health prevents me from taking an active role in the ministry.

In closing my last annotation, I would like to say that I hope the reader has profited from reading as much as I have from editing these two diaries. In no modern work that I have read is there such a clear demarcation between sin and salvation. Together these two diaries shine out like a manual of Thou Shalt Not's.]


I realize, of course, that I am completely insane and trust that everyone, including the Lord in whom, as a last resort, I have come to believe, will forgive me. Sometimes, to be sure, the devil enters into me and takes possession of me and, therefore, I have begun to grow afraid that I may do something drastic and very harmful to myself and others. I have seriously thought about turning myself over to the proper authorities, but I am too weak and too much of a coward to do this, even though I know that it would be best for all concerned.

Of course, since I am insane, I cannot be held legally responsible for any of my actions, past, present, and future, but I fully realize that I still have a moral responsibility for such actions, should they occur, and I ask pardon for them in advance from God, Reverend Perkins, and my mother.

The reasons for my insanity are, of course, readily apparent. I have lived a very sinful life and, on numerous occasions, abused God and his Holy Writ. It is little wonder that Satan saw fit to enter my soul, since I have spent the better part of my life preparing it for him. If nothing can be done to save my soul, I still will derive some joy from thinking that someone may find this diary and profit from my mistakes by avoiding all those too readily apparent sins in which I have too often indulged myself.

It is for this reason and this reason alone that I am going to give these pages to Reverend Perkins.

# *Afterword*

My visits to the Kings continued right up until the afternoon of March 31st, when Edward, as I mentioned in the Preface, handed me his diary. I saw very little of him the last few weeks of his life. He would let me in when I knocked and then disappear upstairs, sometimes greeting me and sometimes not, and, except for the last day, he would wait until I was gone before he came downstairs to bolt the door.

During this time, I always saw Mrs. King in the library, which, as the month passed, became filled with old trunks and suitcases to which I was not permitted to allude. Since some of the trunks looked quite heavy and since they must have been stored in the attic, I assume that Edward was responsible for their being in the library, although it was only Mrs. King who talked about leaving. Why they were there must always remain a mystery.

I should probably mention that on the afternoon of the 31st, Mrs. King seemed more upset than usual and more incoherent than I had ever seen her. I should, I realize, have called in a doctor, even if it meant breaking a trust of long standing. Before I left, she kicked a hole in one of the suitcases and broke into tears, crying over and over again that she should never have done it. What "it" was I never learned, and that, too, must be added to the many mysteries which surrounded the Kings.

Before I left the house, I did manage to calm her down a good deal, and I departed thinking I would see them both again the next day. After leaving the library, I met Edward in the hall. He motioned me into the dining room and handed me the diary, saying simply, "You might enjoy this." That was the last I ever saw of either of them.

The following morning I received a telephone call from Dr. Robinson with whom I had left my telephone number some weeks before. Needless to say, I was terribly stunned and shocked by the news, and I immediately took a taxi to what but the day before had been the King home, and now was nothing more than a heap of smoldering cinders. I was heartbroken and fell down on my knees to pray for the two souls who had perished with the house. I felt that I had in some way betrayed my charges.

When I recovered myself, Dr. Robinson informed me that by the time the fire engines arrived, the house was completely in flames. The firemen were forced to devote all their efforts to saving his house and the one on the other side of the Kings', which had been empty for several months. Nothing could have saved their house. It burned like a tinder box. I blame no one.

Today, the lot on which the King house stood is a garden owned by Dr. Robinson to whom the property was sold. I do not know if he intended the garden as a monument to the Kings, but I like to look at it that way, and I know that both Mrs. King and Edward would have been pleased. I visited the garden a few days ago, with Dr. Robinson's permission, and I sat on a stone bench which must mark the spot where the library sofa stood not too many years before. Memories flooded back over me like waves, and I could not but wonder at the ways of Providence.

ALFRED SYLVESTER PERKINS, D.D.
*Palm Springs, California*
*July 11, 1965*

## About the Author

DOUGLAS MOON was born in 1937 in Fulda, Minnesota, and was brought up in Los Angeles. He received his B.A. and M.A. degrees in English Literature from the University of California at Berkeley, where he is presently completing work for a Ph.D. in English Linguistics. He began the *King Diaries*, his first novel, in the spring of 1964 and not long ago completed a second work of fiction, *Not Louder Shrieks*.